T0405979

WEREWOLF
WC
COUNCIL

WOLFLAND

J. MANOA

E
EPIC
Escape

An Imprint of EPIC Press
EPICPRESS.COM

Wolfland
Werewolf Council: Book #4

Written by J. Manoa

Copyright © 2018 by Abdo Consulting Group, Inc.

Published by EPIC Press™
PO Box 398166
Minneapolis, MN 55439

All rights reserved.

Printed in the United States of America.

International copyrights reserved in all countries.
No part of this book may be reproduced in any form without
written permission from the publisher. EPIC Press™ is trademark
and logo of Abdo Consulting Group, Inc.

Cover design by Candice Keimig & Neil Klinepier
Images for cover art obtained from iStockPhoto.com
Edited by Ryan Hume

LIBRARY OF CONGRESS CATALOGING-IN-PUBLICATION DATA
Names: Manoa, J., author.
Title: Wolfland / by J. Manoa.
Description: Minneapolis, MN : EPIC Press, 2018. | Series: Werewolf council ; #4
Summary: With their secrets revealed, Nate and his fellow werewolves are forced to live in the
    isolated ruins of their town. Meanwhile, Riley, now in exile, awaits the time when her duty
    as a so-called guardian may be required once more.
Identifiers: LCCN 2016946216 | ISBN 9781680765014 (lib. bdg.) | ISBN 9781680765571
    (ebook)
Subjects: LCSH: Friendship—Fiction. | Werewolves—Fiction. | Young adult fiction.
Classification: DDC [Fic]—dc23
LC record available at http://lccn.loc.gov/2016946216

EPICPRESS.COM

For Benjy, Tom, Matt, Kevin, and David 2

PROLOGUE

IT WAS SNOWING AGAIN, NOT THAT THE SNOW ever really stopped in the first place. Private Lily Jenkins walked along the length of temporary fencing that her unit had managed to put up during the first three months of half-decent weather they'd had before the snow started. It was so cold that they couldn't even finish the taller, more secure barrier, let alone the guard towers that were supposed to be placed every two miles around the entire perimeter of the town. Most of those were just concrete blocks by the time construction shut down and all the workers got to go home. Lucky civvies. Better money, and they didn't have to suffer through the endless friggin' winter.

None of the other Wolflands had trouble completing their barrier walls and towers, not even New Mexico, where the Guard had to put down a dozen angry rioters who charged the gate. Of course, those were in nicer places. Just her luck she'd be stuck in the coldest, most isolated town, with a fence low enough that any of the beasts it was supposed to hold back could easily hop over it. No telling what would happen if they got out. Panic, murder, riots, worse than New Mexico, probably worse than any of the other settlements around the country. And this little fence, eight feet of flimsy chain link with a couple of sagging lengths of razor wire, was supposed to prevent that from happening here? Yeah, that makes sense.

She steadied herself before bounding over the narrow stream that ran down the shallow slope. The whole forest looked like a huge lawn mower had come through one strip of land and cut the trees back fifty feet on each side of the fence. It provided a longer sight line for anyone coming and going. Or, it would have, if the guard towers were ready, if the "wall" were more than a weak backstop that shook in a strong breeze, and if those who might possibly approach weren't the size and speed of a damn Buick, getting bigger and faster with every new report.

She heard Lamar stomping along behind her. He paused at the stream and landed with a sort of shuffling plastic noise before lumbering on through. Poor guy had a bum knee from college. So why not station him where monsters could possibly rip it clean off his leg? Sounds about right.

She thought it was strange that she hadn't seen a single wolf in person, not in their "wolfy shape," or whatever it was they called it. She'd only seen them like that on the video feed from the drones that flew along the tree line when the weather allowed. That's right, it snowed so damn much that even robots couldn't survive. No wonder the wolves choose to live here, no right-thinking person would ever come unless they absolutely had to. Like if they were fishermen . . . or insane. So yeah, she thought, it was strange that she hadn't yet seen one in person. She felt the weight of the M16 in her arms. She hadn't fired it since basic. With the way those . . . things . . . moved, probably best she not attempt to relearn marksmanship while on the job.

Funny that despite the cold she still felt sweat beginning on her brow and back. The trudge through ankle-high snow with the gun and the gear, the damn thermals beneath the uniform and tactical vest, the ski mask and goggles, and the combat helmet with its headset and night vision attachment, all made the hundred feet from where the terrain became too rough for the Humvee ride to the possible breach feel like a hike through the Oke Swamp. Except that the predators here were a lot stronger and faster than the gators back home.

She slowed as the break in the fence came into view several feet ahead.

"I think we got it," she hollered over her shoulder to Lamar.

"What?" he shouted back.

She shook her head and continued forward.

The rip started about three feet off the ground and tore all the way to the bottom of the fence. It pulled outward from the bottom, curving like a curtain. The jagged ends showed the links were pulled apart rather than cut. Seemed too small for one of the wolves to fit through, but maybe it was to let a child out or something. If they had children.

She stopped a few feet from the breach. "Here it is," she said, pointing the tear out for Lamar as his bum leg pushed long channels through the snow.

Lamar grunted.

"Imma call it in," Jenkins said. She pulled the small mic closer to her mouth. "West One, this is Private Jenkins. Confirming that breach in mile . . . " She turned to Lamar. "What is this?" she asked, covering the mic.

"Twenty-seven," he replied as a puff of steam through his black mask.

"Breach in mile twenty-seven confirmed, over."

She pressed the headset to her ear to block out the sound of Lamar's panting and the soft breeze blowing down the hill.

"A small one, yeah. Doesn't look like any of them coulda fit through unless it's a little one." She half listened to the response while looking across the ground leading to either side of the hole. "There's a lotta snow out here . . . can't tell if there's tracks or just . . . snow." She nodded and motioned for Lamar to head back toward the Humvee. He sighed heavily before turning. "All right, I'll mention it to the superstar the next time I see 'im. Should be soon." She took one last look over the scene. The wind down the slope carved low waves through the snow. "All right, we're headin' back to ya now. Over and out." She pulled the mic away from her mouth.

"C'mon, big guy," Jenkins said, as she started through the tracks left by Lamar's uneven steps.

"Sooner we get back, the sooner we're outta this damn snow."

"Never stops," Lamar panted.

"That's why we gotta be here," she replied, continuing through the snow, "to make sure nunna them make fer a better place."

A distant noise caused Jenkins to pause for a moment. A howl picked up from the direction of the town. Others joined in to the sound.

"Go, go," she heard from behind as Lamar lumbered quickly toward her.

Jenkins lowered her head and hustled toward the vehicle as the howls rose into a guttural chorus in the distance.

CHAPTER 1

RILEY DUCKED INTO THE ALLEY NEXT TO Forester's Market. A trail of shallow impressions followed her from the other side of the store. Wooden planks blocked off where the door had been ripped from the entrance. Other boards blocked off what had been windows.

She barely felt the cold as she nudged some snow into the footprints behind her, and patted down the snowflakes off the outer rim by her boot. She did this despite knowing that sight wasn't the sense she needed to worry about. There was no way of telling how much of the odorless solution remained on her cloak from its last treatment two months before, when she and others were finally released from the Pointed Hand's compound after extensive and cramped training.

It was the farthest she'd ventured into the town since the night most of the people left. A test, Virgil had called this return during their meeting at a gas station outside of her new town the night before. A test to see if she was as capable as she should be, as capable as she needed to be. Break through the corruption with a symbol of light. "A reminder of who you are and why you choose to fight with us."

Riley gingerly dashed down the next block of boarded shops and storefronts, their contents gutted for anything usable following the initial exodus of all non-Canaanites from the town. She paused again at the corner of Willow and Ahtna. The street ahead glowed with dozens of shades of pristine snow still wafting in the night. The absence of artificial light left the sky filled with an unfathomable number of stars. Even more than she would see during nights when she'd step out from Remy's house far away from town. Farther than . . . his place. The one who started this madness.

She peeked out to see more boards covering the windows along what had been her road. Even the trash can in front of the Chase Bank on the next corner had been removed, its chain with it. They were probably being used for scrap somewhere else, or maybe as barter for something else. She didn't know exactly what happened to the money in the bank, although she couldn't imagine the banks or the government would allow that amount of cash to remain behind the fences of Wolfland. Currency wouldn't be any good here anyway, except for kindling or toilet paper. It wasn't even as valuable as a trash can or length of chain. Those items at least were practical.

The street was clear ahead. Any tracks left from the day had long since been covered by the slow but unceasing snowfall. Down one last block and across one more street before she'd reach the wide face of her old apartment building. Its four floors towered over the smaller buildings before half of its L-shape disappeared behind the ramshackle shops between here and her destination. Windows in the lower two floors had been boarded, as well as those of a couple apartments on the third floor. She squinted to see the corner apartment where she'd lived with her mother until her mother decided to leave, along with all the other unchosen. The glass had been shattered and left. No one wanted to live in that place, not after her. She readied herself for the last run to the corner.

The sound of crunching snow made her freeze. She heard breathing as a pair of Canaanites progressed along the next street, toward the very corner where she needed to be. She backed against the wall behind her, out of their sight. She sank lower in the snow, hoping that the moisture in the air and the lingering solution on her cloak would hide her from the patrol. Snow continued to fall onto her black cloak. Any other person would see nothing but night in a town where the streetlights and windows had gone dark from a lack of power. For Riley, the snow that had fallen on her cloak stood out as clearly as the stars hanging in the sky. She closed her eyes to concentrate on the sound, waiting until she couldn't hear it anymore before peeking around. Long tracks led down the road.

She crept out, keeping her weight even on every part of her foot. Too much pressure would make a deeper print that would take longer to disappear under added snow. She continued along the front of the broken-down storefronts, concentrating on her sloshing footsteps and allowing them to grow louder as she moved away. She looked around the corner of the bank. Long channels through the snow led down the road before cutting across another street. No one else that she could sense. Didn't mean they couldn't sense her. She needed to be quick.

Shallow window ledges led up to the third floor. The climb wouldn't be easy, but it was doable, and hopefully fast. No way to tell if wolves had moved into the apartments surrounding her own, or if they'd be able to smell her through the thin boards that kept out the snow and cold, but she'd come this far, no sense turning back now. She braced herself for the sprint and the climb. Her eyes caught on the bench in front of her building where she had sat with him the night they both first acknowledged Virgil. "Highlander" they had called him, back when they used to communicate through movie references. When they would communicate at all. She drew in one cold breath and darted across the street.

She dashed up the seat and back of the bench as though navigating a pair of steps. She leapt over the snow-covered shrubs lining the building face. She grabbed for the brick arch over the first floor window, her gloved hands gripping through the snow. She pulled herself up as though weightless, planting her weight onto her toes on the one-inch overhang. She jumped for the ledge below the next window and pulled herself up once more. A large crack splintered through the wooden board. The sound of her calm, heavy breathing came through. She climbed onto the next overhang. Only one jump remained.

The glass had been shattered and the blinds ripped off from her living room window. She brushed some sharp slivers from the frame and angled herself through.

"Animals," she muttered to herself.

The word ZEALOTS splayed in sloppy letters greeted her across the wall where pictures of her with her mother and father used to hang. Each letter was half her height and scratched into the plaster in furious strokes.

Did he do this?, she wondered briefly. Her nostrils flared at the thought of someone she'd once cared for, perhaps more than anyone else, breaking into the apartment where she'd lived and destroying everything that marked her place in the town they had shared. How many of the others knew exactly where she lived? How many of *them* would know how to target her?

Fluff from the shredded couch mixed with snow blown through the broken window. Bits of ripped-up fabric were strewn everywhere. A pair of lamps were tossed and shattered against the walls. The smashed television was on top of the stripped couch frame. The dining room table remained intact and in place but with several deep scratches carved into its polished surface. Books, movies, CDs, and magazines were ripped from shelves and littered on the floor. Riley tiptoed through the remnants of her life. The last few pictures her mother left behind had been pushed off the wall to make room for the angry letters now inscribed on it. Broken frames dotted the ground. Some of the pictures were torn in half. Others were crumpled and tossed away. Surveying the destruction once more, it didn't seem like anything was taken.

The metal and wood within the couch, the frames, the wooden table, they all remained, broken but unused, as though the materials themselves were tainted.

"Dammit," she whispered, looking at the ripped and ruined pictures among the shattered glass on the floor. "Well," she sighed, turning toward the hall.

Her clothes were multicolored shreds throughout her bedroom, the dresser drawers piled haphazardly on the ground, their contents rummaged through but mostly contained. Her television and computer were dismantled messes on the ground. The desk drawers were ripped out onto the floor, but the desk itself remained. The bed was shoved sideways against the wall, the mattress flopped over and nearly ripped in half. She sighed into the covering over her face. She'd run almost an hour through the snow, left a dummy trail in that pathetic fence, leapt over, raced across half the town while avoiding patrols, and climbed most of her old building—only to find her home reduced to rubble.

She stepped into the gap where the debris was lowest. One corner of the bottom and largest desk drawer was dented from impact. She crouched next to the drawer, among the destroyed materials that once made up the bulk of her life, and flipped through the stacks of old term papers, birthday cards, and cut-out magazine articles. The drawer never was very well organized, but she roughly knew where everything was. She spotted a gap a couple of inches into the pile. She pushed everything else out of the way. A stack of flung papers would probably be the smallest mess in the place. She pulled the stuffed envelope from the paper stack. The blue and red logo of the old photo printing place ran in a constant loop over the back and front flap of the paper. If he'd been the one to trash the place, at least he had the decency to leave the memories unsoiled.

The two of them, or she and one of *them*, had

bought a pair of disposable cameras because they couldn't find Polaroids like the ones used by Guy Pearce in *Memento*. She flipped through photos of the town the way it was before: the school, the plaza, the museum, her street as it had been, her building, Oak Street Cinema with Antonio's in the background. They meant nothing to her now. They were a part of Wolfland.

Her mother appeared in the next photo, smiling at the camera, with Riley next to her not even attempting to smile. Her mother's hair hung down to her shoulders, dyed black while Riley's had one blond streak in the front. They had the same square chin. A pair of half diamonds formed where her mother's cheekbones met the creases leading down from the top of her nostrils. Riley eyes were half-closed, one cheek pushed slightly up—as though so disinterested in appearing in this photo that she'd give herself a reason to never look at it—while her mother smiled prettily, one arm wrapped over Riley's shoulder to pull her close.

Riley loosened the threads of her cloak collar, pulled open the top buttons, and carefully slid the photograph into the interior breast pocket. She patted it down to make sure it wouldn't get too damaged as she ran back.

She appeared again in the next photo, just as pale and with a blond streak framing her face. She smiled this time, cheeks pulled back to show her teeth in a big, clenched grin. The other person did the same. His hair was a bit longer then, down to his eyes, before he started trying to make it look like Russell Crowe in *Gladiator* or whatever it was. She stared at the photo. They looked so different. Her pale skin and dark features, wide chin and cheeks. Him slightly darker, brown hair and eyes, his straight nose and a long chin pulled outward by his smile. He showed his teeth too. One of his top front teeth was turned a bit to the side, giving it a sharper slope than the others. They used to joke that it was his fang. That *was* the joke.

Was.

Past tense. Like him.

Better to think of him that way. Better that he be dead than what he had become. Dead like her dad, and his dad, and Remy—the victim, the boy who spent his last breaths hanging in the car seat next to her. She'd never taken a picture with Remy. She should have. If she had known what would happen . . . Of course, if she had known what would happen, she probably wouldn't have gotten close to him in the first place. He was an innocent with no part in this . . . conflict . . . this war. He wasn't born into it. Not the way they were.

She turned the photo of her and *him* facedown on the pile.

She stood up. She patted the interior pocket before she closed the buttons on her cloak and tightened the threads across the collar. She turned her back on the wreckage of what had been her life.

ZEALOTS stared at her sideways as she emerged. The word followed her through the ruins of her former home. It watched her climb back out the window and lower herself to hang off the window ledge before dropping onto the one below, with a split second of shock sent through her legs and up her back. It stayed with her all the way through the town she used to consider hers, through the forest, over the fence, and out. And when she closed her eyes that night, she still saw it there, screaming.

Zealots.

CHAPTER 2

NATE STEPPED INTO THE GAS STATION AT THE edge of town. The shelves had long ago been hauled behind the shop for future use. The refrigerators and freezers remained and were no colder than the rest of the shop. He stopped near the counter with its lingering bluish-tinted scents of metal and paper money, the stinging yellow of cigarettes, and the slight red of beef jerky. The rest of the place smelled of old gasoline and spoiled milk left over from the time between when the lights went off and the shop was finally cleared.

The bottom of his robe didn't touch the ground

until he knelt down on the open floor, bracing himself with one large palm. Smells swirled around even as he closed his eyes. He gritted his teeth through the heat that swelled within his bones and laced under his skin. It was gone in a flash. His robe draped over him like a bedsheet. He kept it on as he continued to change into the clothes stashed in his backpack, trying to keep his newly bare skin from contacting the cold.

The robes were a recent addition to accommodate those who wished to change between their forms without suddenly finding themselves naked in the cold. Even with the thin material, the shock of suddenly losing two thick layers of fur—a long top layer over a short undercoat—to naked flesh always reminded Nate of just how strong the elements were. Strong enough that they halted the National Guard in their tracks and kept their eyes-in-the-sky from taking off. Nate exhaled a cloud of steam. He stuffed the robe into his backpack. The robe itself was two separate sets of window curtains stitched together, white and yellow stripes on the sleeves and solid blue through the center. He zipped up the front of his down jacket to right under his chin and pulled his ski mask over his face before folding it back. The rules for approaching the fence stipulated human only, but keeping your face visible was implied. He swung the pack onto his shoulders, tightening the straps for his smaller frame, and stepped out.

He walked between the gas pumps. Their hoses had been removed, along with everything else that the Council had deemed would be useable at some point in the future. The gas itself remained in tanks under the station. The Council publicly declared the gas as an emergency supply, in case the generators ever ran extremely low, but Nate knew that the real reason it hadn't been moved was that the energy needed to move it was greater than the amount of gas left. Every little bit had to be conserved, at least until the cold ended and they could start building. Hopefully.

Wednesday afternoons were Freddie's shift at the little shed next to the inner gate. Nate had tried taking a turn in the six-by-six metal room with one door, darkened windows, and nothing inside but a chair and a small desk. It was quiet and a pretty good place for reading, but there wasn't much reading material left in town, and plenty of other places were quiet without being tiny metal cans.

The inner fence, as they called it, was only six feet high and barely stretched farther than the road out of town. Anyone could easily climb or walk around it; however, the Council decided that as a sign of good faith, no one would do so. They also determined that anyone who stepped beyond the fence had to appear human, despite the ten-minute walk between the inner and outer fences being only a one-minute run. Nate understood the intention—follow orders, make concessions, win favor in order to ask for it back later—but he couldn't help but suspect that Ulrich really decided on that rule because he was never the one who had to make that ten-minute walk in the wind and snow. Nate unlatched the fence and yanked one side as hard as he could to get it rolling. The lock swung back and forth as the fence opened. He nodded to the shed as he stepped through. He figured Freddie would be watching from inside. Nothing else to do.

Nate stashed his hands in his jacket pockets as he walked. The road ahead rose to the outline of the high fence. Only an inch of snow had fallen the night before—much better than the six dumped on the town last week. The Council arranged to clear the first half mile beyond the inner fence and left the rest of it for the Guard, who would never move through the outer fence unless given a good reason. Clearing the road was not a good reason. Again, Ulrich wasn't the one who had to trudge through the snow.

Ice hung from tree branches like glass fangs. If Nate concentrated on the snow on the trees or the road he could see the steam of melting, as though the treetops were burning. There was an odd comfort in the clouds of cold breath, the mist, the melting, as though some part of how he saw the world persisted in both of his forms. If only the rest of the world could understand that, then maybe he wouldn't have to take this walk.

The makeshift barracks with its mismatched bricks came into view through the ten-foot-high chain link lined with barbed wire and a double gate that cut across the road. The Guard had focused on securing each way out of town, while other portions of the surrounding fence were all but neglected. Ulrich had stated that he believed this was part of the trust their kind needed with the outside world, that even though those inside could easily leave, they didn't. It was an opportunity for trust and cooperation between the two peoples. Nate assumed it was simply where the Guard decided to station themselves, mostly out of convenience and self-preservation. Part of him also liked to think that since no wolf would take the road to leave, maybe the gates were to keep those outside from coming in—those he'd heard about who'd attempted to attack settlements in other parts of the country—rather than those inside from coming out. At least then there was some pretense of protection and not just isolation.

Nate held up one hand as the two guards posted at both sides of the gate came into view. They wore brown helmets of desert camouflage with rolls of thick fabric. They were allowed to keep their black masks pulled up and over their noses. They also had automatic weapons. Nate stopped his approach. He put both his hands out. "Wallace," he yelled, "eight-one-one-twenty-four-eight-forty-two!"

One of the guards leaned to speak into a comm set mounted on his shoulder. Nate took a moment to look around. The white of the ground nearly matched that of the clouds. He looked back to see the guard waving him on.

While most of the soldiers had to remain in the barracks, with red bricks filling in where the concrete blocks had run out, the houses lining the road were taken over by private contractors hired to construct the fence. Of course, most of them left for the winter, leaving a half-finished fence, empty houses, and an overstuffed barracks. Nate halted a few feet from where the gate broke into the asphalt and the ground around it. As he waited, he knocked the snow from the treads of his shoes, trying not to make eye contact with the soldiers. Further down the road, around a few turns, maybe five more minutes driving, or fifteen for him, was his own house. Unless it had been burned down by now. No way of knowing. He heard the barracks door swing open and the crunch of boots on the snow.

"Hey," Private Jenkins said as she approached, her mask under her chin. "It's the world's most famous werewolf."

"What?"

"Saw you on the news," she continued. She had heavy cheeks with a little mole just to the right side of her mouth and her voice was surprisingly soft for someone in her position.

Nate shrugged. "We agreed it'd be best that no one else be identified as . . . one of us. In case the time comes when it's, you know, okay. Or," he added snidely, "so that I'm the only one people want to kill."

Jenkins came to a few feet from the other side of the gate. She kept her gloved hands steady on the M16 strapped over her shoulder, but at least her finger wasn't on the trigger. "That's what it's like being a celebrity," she said, "as many people wanna kill ya as wanna cheer for ya. Like that for soldiers too."

"I guess that's true," Nate said.

"You people know any more about New Mexico?"

Nate shook his head. "Hard to get information in here."

"I heard somewhere that yer people can sense what others're thinkin'. Like with . . . what are they . . . phermonds?"

"Pheromones," Nate replied, "but what you're

talking about is hormones. They're like reading facial expressions, though more reliable I guess."

"So what am I thinkin' now?"

"It's not psychic and it only works when we're . . . changed."

"That's too bad. It would make explainin' things so much easier. Hey," she said without pausing, "is it true what you said on that interview, that you people own the town?"

"The original charter establishes it as a sanctuary, if that's what you mean."

"But it ain't like one of those Indian reservations with the casinos and cheap cigarettes."

"We wouldn't have enough power to run any casinos, and there are no visitors. I'm also pretty sure the smell of cigarettes would drive us all mad."

"And we wouldn't want that, right?" Jenkins said with an ominous laugh. "Report made it look nice though. Everyone outside all the time, no one working, yer people walking around like it's some kinda dog park 'r something."

"Something like that."

"I'd kinda like to see it sometime, if you people would allow it."

Nate took a moment before answering. "I can ask."

"Eh, don't worry about it." Jenkins waved her hand in dismissal, "I mean, it'll probably be a few years before you people get any kinda formal recognition, if you ever do. You heard anything about that?"

"No," Nate said again.

"Not even in the report?"

"I didn't get to see it."

"Oh, right. I thought maybe what's-'er-face mentioned it to you, the reporter that had the bird whack her in the face that one time. Did ya see that video?"

"A long time ago."

"Well, apparently there're some people, not many but a few, that are demanding recognition and rights fer you people, like what the Indians get. Might be kinda good. Then at least maybe we can head home."

"Yeah," Nate said, half listening, "home."

"So," Jenkins continued, "I suppose yer here about the supply truck?"

Nate nodded.

"It's gonna be late."

Nate shrugged. Late again. "Any estimated time?"

"Next week maybe. You people are good at hunting and nature stuff though, right? Might hafta be stingy with the water but you can still feed yerselves."

Nate put his hands out to the world around them. "It's winter."

"Well that's kinda yer fault for choosing to live up here, ain't it? I mean, all this snow. You should kinda expect shortages."

"We're a bit new to this particular situation," Nate replied, trying to limit the amount of venom in his words.

"Maybe you people coulda planned a bit better then."

Nate sighed.

"I keep saying that," Jenkins said. "'You people.' Is there somethin' different I can say other than 'people'?"

Nate shook his head. "So," he said, moving on, "supplies . . . Monday? Tuesday?"

"Yeah 'bout Monday or Tuesday. Maybe Thursday."

Nate sighed once more. His breath was a cloud in front of him. "All right."

"Somethin' serious though." Jenkins took one step closer to the gate. "We found another breach in the fence around mile twenty-five . . . eight . . . in the twenties. We're gonna need y'all to make sure none o' yer types got loose."

"All right. I'll ask that we initiate another count once I get back. Do you need us to help with the fence?"

"Nah, we got it," Jenkins replied with a confident nod. "We can do ya that favor."

"Thanks."

"Since yer a celebrity an' all."

"Anything else?" Nate asked.

"That's about it. Maybe head back out here after the count is finished and let me know if any of yer folks are out there. Better we know now than after somethin' bad happens. Not that all yer people are bad but, ya know."

"It might take a few hours."

Jenkins raised one hand under the barrel of her rifle. "We ain't goin' nowhere," she said.

"I know," Nate replied. "All right, I'll be back later."

"We'll be here."

Nate nodded as he turned. "I know that too," he muttered to himself.

He heard Jenkins slush in the snow on the other side of the gate. He pulled the ski mask over his face, stuffed his hands back into his pockets, and started back to the town. He was the only one who ever had to make this long walk in the cold. The only one who had to speak with the soldiers posted with their guns or carry bad news from the outside world back in with him. This was his reward for being the world's most famous werewolf.

CHAPTER 3

THE FOUNTAIN HAD BEEN DRY SINCE THE DAY after Nate made his worldwide television debut, destroying a two-hundred-year-old secret agreement between humanity and Fenrei. *His people.* He'd done so right in front of that very same dry fountain he passed almost every day after walking back from the outer western gate, running to an abandoned insurance office on Cedar a block from the plaza, changing, and then walking to the museum. There was always a Council meeting to attend. Possibly because the situation within the fence was always changing. Probably because there was nothing else for the councilors to do.

Nate saw a pair of wolves walking through the park. One was big and bulky, angular, the other a bit thinner with rounder shoulders and legs. Male and female. Probably not much older than he was. The female continued on as the male stopped to scoop a handful of snow. He took a second to pack it into a loose ball. He waited while the female kept walking. He barked something at her. The female turned. The snowball flew weakly over the female's left shoulder. She stared at him as though unimpressed by this game. She sighed as she turned to continue up the path. The male followed with a shrug. Nate exhaled one slow, streaming cloud, tucked his hands under his backpack straps, and continued on.

Wooden posts poking through the snow marked land sectioned off for future garden projects. The ground was too frozen to begin now, but it would thaw as it got warmer next year. There wasn't nearly enough land to feed all of the two hundred sixty-eight who remained in the town, but enough that, in theory, they would be less dependent on outside supplies.

"Good morning, Ambassador Wallace," Nate heard from across the road. A small woman in a thick, orange jacket and yellow hat waved to him. A wolf behind her covered her entire shoulder with one hand. He swung his head low and away.

Nate raised one hand back to them.

The woman held onto one of the wolf's fingers. Her happy expression quickly dulled as they continued on, passing what used to be Southland Snow and Hiking Supplies. The plain wood of the new door stood out against the dark green and white paint of the old store. The shop was still empty, but at least none of the glass and splintered wood remained.

Next to the hiking supply shop was what used to be Nicolai's Bakery. Mr. Clarkson and his family had moved in after his house had been broken into during the panic ten weeks before. Clarkson said that the intruders busted through the door lock and grabbed a couple of small statues that looked more valuable than they were. The two guys were in the process of carrying Clarkson's television out when he and his wife emerged from the bedroom. One look at the claws and fangs and the robbers dropped the television to run. They even left a pistol behind. The Council agreed to let the family stay in the shop until repairs reached their section of town by the school.

Nate surveyed the rest of the street as he continued on. Repairs would continue through the winter until the weather heated up and they could get back to the crops. Next would be livestock, both in the forest and in the town. It still wouldn't be enough to feed everyone, but it was another gesture of cooperation to the humans who surrounded them. Eventually, Ulrich had argued, they'd demonstrate that this town could manage itself, even if none of the others could. These people, who chose to remain behind a fence they could easily breach, could be trusted. That's when they would start asking for more advanced items: electric generators, restoration of their connection to the state's water supply instead of piping it from the streams, maybe even a lifting of the telecommunication restriction. "Restore some normalcy," Ulrich said during a meeting last month when he first outlined his plan. "Just as things were before." But, he had warned those in the room, that could only work if they all cooperated.

Nate turned at the driveway from Cedar into the lot between the museum and the plaza. He walked out onto the asphalt, a striking black surface among the snowfall everywhere else. A small rotation of workers was assigned to shovel the lot and the steps in the morning because this place, out of everywhere else, had to be clean. It was a symbol of their achievements and the foundation of their community. At least, that's what Ulrich said. The crowd seemed to agree.

Nate paused to compare the two humans facing each other across the gap in the relief carved into the walls flanking the museum steps. Would they eventually change one or both of them to reflect their new situation? Or was that the point of the relief in the first place: to depict the two species living together in secret as they had for centuries? Nate continued on.

Voices echoed from the main gallery as soon as he entered the museum. Meetings had been moved from the back as a sign of greater openness, both within the town and among the community itself. Nate leaned toward the doors to see who was in attendance.

"Good morning, Ambassador Wallace," said the old lady with the huge glasses sitting behind the reception desk. "Any news on the next shipment?"

"Nothing good," he replied, continuing toward the doors. He saw the small circle gathered off-center from where the information block stood under Leonard the blue whale.

"That's a shame," the woman said.

His eyes caught on the plaque at the side of the entrance as he approached. He lingered a moment over the names of Patrick Wallace and Clarence McKnight. He half expected McKnight's name to be scratched out. Maybe his father's as well. He moved back toward the reception desk.

The old woman looked up at him over the thick rim of her giant glasses. Her hair was pure white, like the snow outside. Her lips were brittle with cracks.

"I'm sorry," he said, stopping in front of her, "but I can't remember your name."

"Well, you were very, very young when we first met," she replied, eyes almost as big as the lenses over them. "Annabelle Moore."

"Annabelle," he said, nodding.

"Annie," she offered, "ever since I was a little girl."

"Promise I'll remember it this time."

"I'm sure you will, Ambassador," she replied.

Nate couldn't tell if she was being sarcastic or sincere as he paced through the door.

A trio of wolves were spaced among the small gathering. Ulrich's face appeared between the backs toward the door. He seemed to eye Nate during his entire approach through the gallery as others in the circle talked. A couple of others whom Nate recognized from previous meetings turned toward him. They turned away just as quickly.

" . . . we clean up the school so they'll at least have someplace they can go," said the man at eight o'clock to Ulrich's twelve and Nate's six. "Even just the hall and a pair of classrooms."

"There are more important things to focus on now," said one of the others who turned when Nate entered. The wolf at his side was a full two feet taller than he was. Each of the wolves was that much bigger, give or take a few inches.

"Children need education," the first man continued, "and this is finally a time when we can teach them about their own heritage and culture without threat."

"What children?" said a woman on the other side of the room. "All, what, twenty who remain?"

"Clearing the school would be a sign that we're committed to maintaining a high standard in our community. It can be as much a symbol as this museum is—"

Ulrich put his hand up. The man stopped talking.

"Cleanup has been slower than any of us had hoped," he said. Shayera stood half a step back from his side. Nate couldn't tell if she had seen him there or not. "Remember that we made the choice together to begin in the center and work our way outward. We'll get to the school eventually, but for now any classes can be conducted here." A few among the crowd met Nate with stern looks. They parted to give him room opposite Ulrich. "The museum would perhaps be a more suitable location for the education you speak of."

The man nodded, "I understand, High Councilor."

Maier stood straight up a few places to Nate's right, a wolf between the two of them. It wasn't Zarker.

"Ambassador Wallace," Ulrich said, lifting himself as he spoke to project across the gap. The honorary title was his idea, a veiled way of separating Nate from any real influence among the Council. "Any news of the outside world?"

Nate took a long breath. "Supply shipment is delayed due to snow," he said. "It'll be at least until next Monday." There was disapproval among the group. "Most likely after next Thursday." Disappointed glances landed on him.

Ulrich tilted his head. He stared at Nate as though this news were his fault—because it was. "Well," Ulrich said, "looks like rationing will have to continue for the time being."

A slight grumble rose from the circle.

"We all knew the first winter would be difficult,"

Ulrich added, "but we are a resourceful people. We will make do with what we have until the spring. After that, we'll be much better provided for next year." Ulrich looked across to Nate, then to the others before continuing. "This isn't a situation we could have planned for."

Grunts of agreement arose.

"Is that all, Ambassador?" Ulrich asked. The title's ironic tone was also his idea.

"There's another hole in the fence, somewhere around the twenty-mile marker." More angry looks came Nate's way. "Private Jenkins has asked that we initiate a count to assure that none of our people escaped."

"Who?"

"A guard at the western gate," Nate said, reminding Ulrich about Private Jenkins's identity for the dozenth time.

"Right, your liaison," Ulrich chided.

"Yes," Nate answered dryly, "my liaison."

"Well then," Ulrich continued, looking around

the room, "I suppose it's only right that the spokes-man of our kind be the one to assure the Guard of the Nation that our kind hasn't violated the terms of our latest agreement with theirs."

Stifled laughter snorted from a few others.

"They expect it to be done quickly." Nate did very little to mask the resentment in his tone. "I need at least a few others."

"So you've thought this through ahead of time," Ulrich said with a nod, leaving the "for once" unsaid. "Shayera, please assist Ambassador Wallace on his head count of all those who remain in our town."

"Yes, High Councilor," Shayera said with a quick nod. Her eyes remained straight ahead, as though looking to the wall behind Nate.

"I'll need a few more," Nate replied. "There are two hundred sixty-eight of us."

"Well, there's what . . . sixteen in here," Ulrich said. "That should make things a little easier."

Nate's jaw clenched.

Ulrich waved his hand in dismissal. "Recruit whoever you wish for this task." He leaned to speak with Shayera loud enough that everyone else could hear. "Report your findings to me prior to meeting with the Ambassador's liaison."

"Yes, High Councilor," she replied again.

"Are you satisfied, Ambassador?" Ulrich stared across the circle. Nate stared back, trying to match the thinly veiled vitriol in the old man's eyes. He felt the disapproving gazes of the others—not all, but enough that he knew he wasn't welcome.

"No. But it'll do," Nate replied before turning his back on the group and walking away.

CHAPTER 4

THE HOWL SHOOK OFF THE BUILDINGS AS though echoing through a low canyon. Nate took a couple of quick breaths before letting out a second long, sustained sound. Others replied from several blocks away.

Shayera crossed her arms as they waited for the few occupants of the southeastern area of the town to come out from behind their makeshift doors. A pair of humans and one wolf wearing a corncob-patterned robe exited from different buildings four blocks away from the plaza, approaching the small bridge that divided the larger northern side from the smaller southern side. The wolf nodded as he passed, a rush in his step to join the rest of the residents in and around the dry fountain for yet another head count. It was the third in as many weeks. The result was never different.

Nate took a moment to check the buildings on the next street. He sensed a fresh wooden plank on the corner, broken glass under a window, but nothing living inside.

"Haven't cleared that far yet," Shayera said as a rolling rumble.

"Check anyway," Nate replied, the cold making it even harder to manipulate a long mouth that wasn't made for words. She huffed before swinging into motion. "Not like we have anything better to do," Nate remarked.

They wandered down the next road, smelling old grease from the abandoned auto shop and the river water three more blocks away. The buildings had mostly been cleared of rubble, but repairs—boards over the doors and windows—hadn't yet been made on any but the first building.

"Check more?" Shayera asked with a hint of annoyance.

Nate took one last, long sniff of air. Shayera was a thin, red pulse under a backpack full of musty clothes and a robe made from a bedsheet with red and blue circles, squares, and stripes that overlapped each other into purple. He saw it all as a dull, gray fabric over a warm-hued form.

"We can go," he said.

Shayera groaned as she turned.

"What?"

Shayera said nothing as she stalked away.

They made sure to wind back through the town streets on their way to the plaza, checking the air for any stragglers still hiding in their new homes. A distant howl echoed from the west as Zarker finished his own circle around the other side of the cleared-out area of town.

"Don't like this," Shayera muttered.

"I know," Nate replied. He motioned for Shayera to head down the road toward the southern entrance into the plaza.

"Don't like it," she said again, "at all."

"Too bad," Nate replied to her back.

"Right for once," she seemed to whisper.

"What does that mean?"

Shayera continued on.

"What does that mean?" he asked once more.

She stopped her steps. The melting snow was a white mist around her. He didn't need to see her expression to read the bubbling resentment that followed them from the museum to Zarker's little hovel behind an old strip mall on the northern edge of town, and then to the southern side.

"It is too bad," she replied. "All of it. Too bad."

Nate stared at her for a moment. He sensed the large crowd gathering a few blocks away. As much of a hassle as the counts were, they worked to break the monotony of daily life within the fence. The scents of old dirt and grease caught his attention, approaching from the west. Zarker ran down the street with another wolf behind him. "Done?" Nate called as Zarker's massive glowing presence drew closer.

He grunted in affirmation.

"Should change," Nate said, "can talk better that way." He motioned toward an alley behind one of the boarded up buildings on the corner. Zarker and the other wolf, Barber, positioned themselves at either side of the alley. "Come on," Nate snarled when Shayera didn't move. She huffed once more before following.

Nate left the others at the end of the alley as he continued down. He dropped his bag a good distance away, far enough to feel comfortable changing both forms and clothes. He pulled the ends of his robe shut and braced for the flash of heat that ripped through his body. The collapsing of bones into themselves still caused him to cringe and shake. Tiny spasms continued as he opened his eyes, fingers clutching at fabric that bunched over his feet.

"—never happen this way," he heard Shayera say in a clear voice from over his shoulder.

Nate crouched to open the bag, tugging the robe over himself.

"The video would have blown over like UFOs and Bigfoot."

"No," Zarker growled back. "Not this time."

Nate pulled his shoes and socks from the bag first, then dug through the clothes inside.

"Would have talked," Barber added. He'd witnessed the conflict when Zarker came face-to-face with Father Vigilius and the blackrobes' newest member. Or possibly their oldest, as she'd been born into their ranks.

"The Council would have found a way to make the stories disappear," protested Shayera. "Like they had before. Ulrich would've found a way. Worked with the others." Nate heard the loud zip of Shayera yanking her bag open.

Nate fumbled to cover as much of himself as possible while getting dressed.

"No more hiding," Zarker said, his voice more that of an animal than a man.

Nate kept his head down as they spoke. He saw the shuffling under the robe. He couldn't help thinking how awkward this situation would have been a few months ago. Changing his clothes in an alley behind a building two blocks from the center of town with nothing but a thin robe from being completely exposed. To the cold. To the world. Funny that he was still modest after showing himself to everyone.

"Oh, c'mon, Robert," Shayera replied, in a tone that seemed as irritated as it was familiar, "we're still hiding. Only now everyone else knows exactly where to find us: the army, the Order, anyone."

Nate bent down to stuff the robe into his empty bag.

"The Order is still out there," Shayera said. "No matter how much we ignore them. They will come back."

"Let them," Zarker growled.

"Of course you would say that," she replied. "What about the rest of us? Those who can't, or won't, fight? What about them?"

Nate quickly zipped the bag closed.

"Better to die free."

"Free," Barber echoed. Neither he nor Zarker wore a robe.

"This isn't freedom!" Shayera replied. Nate peeked over his shoulder. She'd turned to face Zarker at the end of the alley. Her robe hung loose from her body, one end swinging as she flung her arms in wide gestures. "This is a prison camp! What we had before—"

"Was fear," Zarker snarled.

"Was choice!" Shayera continued.

Nate slung the bag over his shoulders as he turned. He felt the weight tug at his body.

"We could live as we wanted within certain restrictions. Might not have been the best selection of choices but at least we had some." Shayera's robe dipped as she bent to grab her shirt from over her pack. Nate turned away. "More than we do now."

"Still have choice," said Zarker. "Choose to stay inside."

Shayera knelt to remove her jacket from the bag. "Really?" she said, pausing to look up at Zarker, "you think you can just wander off whenever you please?"

Zarker simply growled.

She reached into the bottom of the pack. "You wouldn't last a week out there. As soon as anyone spotted you—on foot, from the sky, anywhere—they'd be after you in a second."

Zarker growled again.

"Even if you tried to blend in you wouldn't pass." She zipped the jacket up. "Shit. You barely passed for human when we were surrounded by them."

Zarker snorted heavily.

"And once you were caught out there, or killed, they would find out who you were, where you came from, and it would all come back to us. The rest of us would have to suffer. Again."

"I get it!" Nate screamed. "I get it all right?" Shayera spun around. Her eyes were giant with surprise. "It's my fault! It's all my fault!" Shayera looked away. Barber did as well. "This . . . prison," Nate said, gesturing at the town around them and the fence around it. "No food. Little power. No communication. Limited water. My fault. I get it." One of the bag straps slipped from his shoulder. He pulled it back up. "I'm an idiot, okay? I wasn't thinking and my actions made everyone else suffer."

Nate stepped toward the others. Shayera slid away, shaking, muttering something he couldn't hear.

"Everyone else would be better off if I had never done anything," he said.

Shayera continued shaking her head. Barber cast his view downward. Even Zarker had lowered himself nearer to the ground, almost bowing. "Better if

I had never lived," Nate added quietly. His lips had trouble moving. "I get it."

"I'm sorry," Shayera whispered, "I didn't mean—"

"But you know what? None of that matters. None of it." Nate tugged at the bag straps to tighten them again. The others quivered before him: Shayera with her model height and chiseled figure, Zarker with his mane of wild spikes and legs big enough to hide his head behind. "We live with it," Nate said again. "Everything we did. Everything that led us here. The choices we made. Every moment of every day." His voice grew quieter as he spoke, rattling through his throat, shaking almost as much as they were. "We live with it."

"I'm . . . I'm sorry," Shayera muttered.

"You shouldn't be," Nate replied as he walked to the road passed her. "You're not the one who messed up." He stepped around the corner, away from the plaza. "Add one to whatever number you get. I'm going home."

"The Council ordered you to conduct—"

"The Council didn't order me to do anything. Never has."

"The High Councilor—"

"Screw the High Councilor."

"High Councilor Ulrich speaks for the Council," Shayera said, following Nate as he walked down the street, "which speaks for the—"

"Then screw the Council," Nate said.

The footsteps behind him stopped. He moved on.

The apartment was dark when he arrived, as it usually was at this time in the afternoon. It made the room feel even emptier than usual, hiding the blank walls behind boxes stacked two and three high.

It would probably be an hour before his mother returned from the count. That should be enough time.

The labels flashed under his eye level: "study," "Mom's bedroom," "Nate's stuff." The weight of the upper ones had started pushing dents into those below, the "living room" and "garage" boxes.

Six weeks prior, the whole building had to be cleared before the Council allowed anyone to move in. Elders and those with young children got first priority in housing of course, coincidentally including both Ulrich and Maier, who moved into Riley's old building three blocks closer to the town center. Nate and his mother had managed to spend a few days in their house, but once the plans for the fence were finalized, they were forced to leave much of their stuff behind and move into the town. The next two weeks were spent sleeping under a thick blanket on an empty mattress among the boxes and leftovers of what used to be a tax center. The new door wasn't installed until an hour after they had pulled their belongings from the back of the military transport truck that shuttled them into town.

He put his hands out as he turned through the

darkened room, which was still too new for him to memorize. He tapped around to find the passage between the wall and the couch that they'd barely managed to fit through the door. He traced over the bathroom door in the corner and over to the one for his room. At least he had a door here.

His mother had left her bedroom door open on the other side of the room. He opened his own carefully, making sure not to bang it against the armrest of the couch.

Most of his stuff remained boxed. Some clothes hung off the cardboard rim. A few garments littered the floor next to the bare mattress. A thick comforter formed a mound at the center of the mattress. His two pillows were pushed up against the corner of the room. A pair of boxes held up a third in the opposite corner. Inside were old books and pictures and DVDs, stuff he didn't need, or couldn't use, but couldn't part with. Nate walked around to the side of his bed, kicking a pair of jeans he'd worn the day before, and fell onto the mattress.

He rolled onto his side, facing the box with T-shirts and a jacket hanging halfway out. Still folded inside were his warm-weather clothes, light sweaters, shirts he'd received as gifts from the only person whom he trusted to recognize his taste. Riley. Her name came into his mind like a confession. He kicked his shoes onto the floor, where they landed with a muffled thud, and folded his legs up. He pulled the comforter to just under his eyes. The whole thing smelled vaguely of fabric softener and sweat. He closed his eyes to the darkness.

This was transition. This was building. Building required knocking down. It required breaking what wasn't working to replace it with what will. Loss and uncertainty to make room for gain and comfort. It makes noise and clutter and dust. Building is work and pain and, best of all, temporary. Then, after the building is done, that's when something better arises. Something clean and new. A new beginning. For him, for his mother, for everyone. They will be better that way. Independent. Free. Accepted among their own kind and sheltered from those who threaten them. This . . . this horrible ending for a better beginning . . . this is what he'd asked for that day. He'd asked for them to be safe. All of them. Safe and free and . . . alone.

He pulled the comforter up until he felt it push the short hairs on the side of his head. He saw nothing but a solid black when he shut his eyes and softer, lighter black when he opened them. He felt himself shaking. It wasn't from cold. It wasn't from heat. He still shook. Every part of him. He squeezed his eyes until he felt his skin overlap at the corners. His breathing filled the cocoon over and around him. The shaking continued.

This wasn't transition. This wasn't building. This wasn't safe or new. This wasn't a beginning or independence or acceptance or any of that other nonsense he told himself to justify what he'd done.

This was destruction. This was shunning. This was the loss of everything he'd ever known and cared about. Everyone. This wasn't temporary. This was life, life as it would always be. His every action these last few months: the incident on the night he changed, running through town with Riley over his shoulder, running again from Antonio's after attacking that waiter in front of a dozen witnesses, screaming at reporters around the fountain. He'd been forced at first, but he'd chosen the rest, and it all led him here.

He felt his teeth rattling as he shook. He hugged his arms around himself. He pulled his knees up to his elbows. He couldn't escape the cold.

This was all his own fault.

This destruction.

This exile.

This loss.

His fault.

CHAPTER 5

"You gonna be okay without me?"

"Fine."

"All right, just remember, if you get overwhelmed then too bad because I'm not coming back until tomorrow."

"Umm . . . okay," the new guy said with a blank look, which made Riley chuckle silently.

Riley hurried past the three remaining customers. The last man in line tapped his foot and checked his watch repeatedly as the next person stepped to the register. Riley stifled another chuckle at such a display of impatience when whatever he was in a rush for was meaningless.

A large Buick was parked in the handicapped stall in front of the coffee shop. The proper permit hung from the rearview mirror up front. None of the people inside seemed to be disabled. But some things are hard to tell by appearance. Doesn't mean they are or aren't those things. Also doesn't make it any less shocking or any less of a betrayal to find out what they really are. She walked between the Buick and the SUV next to it, keeping her hands in her pockets as she crossed the parking lot.

A gust of wind blowing snowflakes across her line of sight reminded her to pull her hood up. The fur-lined fabric pushed the front of her hair down to just above her eyebrows. The hood was like the plastic leg cast before it: she needed to be seen using it more than she needed to use it. She'd been told to blend in.

The stores provided more light than the streetlamps. The evening rush just ended and already it had been dark for several hours. Snow drifted through the bright yellow glow of restaurants, convenience stores, and sporting goods shops. Cars drove slowly over the damp but not yet frozen roads. That time would come, not yet, but it would come. That's why it was important to enjoy this period, when the coldest, darkest days were still an idea, a "someday," not a reality. Yet inevitability made this free period, this time before, difficult to appreciate. After all, whatever is done during this time will be meaningless.

She removed her gloved hands briefly to place them over her nose and mouth as she walked. She breathed out to take away some of the chill over her face. The days were growing colder and would continue to be cold for another couple of months, but it had also been a while since her last communion. Some of the effect had worn off. She waited until hidden in the gap between streetlights to let her vision light up the neighborhood. At least she still had that. Things could be worse. She blinked the light away while continuing down two blocks. She turned left on the next corner. Things will be worse.

Eight little snow-covered fir trees lined the front yard. Behind them was a stretch of light with darker black patches. She followed the walkway that led from the drive and around the house. The fence clattered as she lifted the latch. An overhead light clicked on automatically. It made the snow a dull yellow with patches of brown. The house was blue in the day but yellow in the light. The light didn't reach the rear of the house. Her two keys came on a ring with a small compass attached to it, inscribed with the words "Green Rocks Wilderness Lodge." She used the little bit of reflected light and her familiarity to open the door and then ran her hand up the wall until the switch flipped up.

Riley scraped the bottom of her shoes against the rough mat inside. After leaving the shoes to hopefully dry before the next morning, she placed her coat on the last in a line of hooks behind the door and ran her hand through her hair. That was her favorite part of having it short: it took seconds to dry. All together she estimated that she'd probably spent about two years of her life before now just drying her hair. Of course, it took longer to dry now than it did after she'd first moved in, when this odd urge to cleanse herself after the confines of the Pointed Hand caused her to borrow the landlord's electric razor and shave off all but half an inch. She actually wanted to take it all the way down, as though starting clean, but that was Dove's thing.

She walked through the narrow kitchen that came with everything she'd need for her life alone. Her view caught on the window over the sink. She'd felt strange seeing herself with such short hair after spending her entire life with it long. She was expecting something like Natalie Portman in *V for Vendetta*. Instead, her wider chin made her look more like the lady from *Empire Records* who wasn't Liv Tyler or Renee Zellwegger. It was only after pondering how long it would take to grow back that she realized she didn't even think about the three long scars that he'd scratched into her face. She'd grown so accustomed to them being there, yet accustomed to not thinking about where they came from, that they'd become as much as part of her identity as the long black hair. She barely even thought about them until catching the occasional stare and a quick look away. Car accident, she'd tell the few people who mustered up the courage to ask. There was no reason for her to lie, but even less of a reason to tell the whole truth. This version of herself was so much easier to handle.

The short hallway between the kitchen and bedroom crossed between two doors: one to the bathroom, the other to the rest of the house. The second was bolted on both sides, an agreement of mutual distrust between her and the landlord.

A pair of gym bags sat on the floor of the open closet. Riley scooped up the remote from atop the bedside dresser. The buzz of the old television was cut off by the screech of tires and a blast of gunshots of some action movie. The airy comforter nearly swallowed her up after falling into the bed. She pushed down the pillow-like comforter enough to get her head above it all. The movie must have been old—Bruce Willis still had hair.

A solid knock from the hallway covered a tinny explosion from the television. Riley rocked back against the mattress. She sprang up and nearly over rotated on her landing, underestimating the force she could generate with such little movement. She'd been out of practice since her last run northeast toward town. Stumpvale. Wolfland. The Quarantine Zone. Area Fifty-wolf. Whatever it was called now. The forest and hills took three hours for her to cover on foot. The barricades and checkpoints made it unreachable by car.

"Yes?" she asked as she approached the door into the main part of the house.

She heard the lock on the other side click open. She looked around quickly to assure she didn't have anything incriminating out. Not that she really owned anything incriminating other than the wrist blade that she kept at the bottom of her backpack. She pulled the bolt back and pushed the door open.

"Evenin', Riley," Mr. Crawford said. He was only a couple of inches taller than she was. The lines on his forehead, cheeks, and around his eyes hung like those of a bulldog and a few dark marks rode the overlaps in his neck, yet his eyes were the color of mossy rocks through stream water and his silver-gray hair was so thick it looked like he could break the end of his comb off. He placed one of his thin arms on the shelf of *National Geographic* magazines, screwdrivers, and other "useful things" he kept next to the door. "How are you tonight?" he asked.

"I'm fine," Riley replied as pleasantly as possible. "How are you?"

"Oh, fine. I was just going to make some soup and thought you might like a bowl."

"It's okay, Mr. Crawford. There's some work I need to do tonight."

"Oh," a look of surprise came over the old man's face, "decided to go back to school?"

"Some other time. The year's half done anyway."

"I'm sure you can catch up without much trouble."

"I wasn't much of a student."

"Well, we don't have much of a school," he said with a hearty laugh.

There was a chirp from Riley's pocket.

"Are you smuggling birds?" Crawford asked.

"It's my phone."

Crawford stood blinking. He motioned for her to answer.

"It's fine, probably the new guy at work can't find the stirring straws or something."

"That sounds important."

"It's not."

Crawford shrugged. His arms dropped to his sides. They seemed especially thin compared to the round belly that hung over the belt to his jeans.

"Secret admirer?" he said with raised eyebrows.

Riley chuckled. "Doubt it."

"Sure you don't want some soup? Not even a

little? Probably better than microwave pizza, or whatever it is you have planned for dinner."

"I'm okay, Mr. Crawford," Riley said with a nod, "really I am."

She could see the large portrait on the living room wall, a black-and-white shot of Crawford, back when he was barrel-chested and dark-haired, with a small blond woman next to him and a little girl in a frilly white dress at their feet. She noticed others during her tour on the day she moved in. He and the woman moved into color pictures, their hair grayer and shapes rounder. The little girl always remained little. She was always black and white. She wanted to ask what happened to them, but never did. It was best to not get involved.

Her phone chirped once again.

"Drink lids," Riley said without a moment's hesitation.

Crawford's hearty laugh filled the doorway.

"All right," he said, "I see there's no persuading

you with soup. But if you change your mind there should be plenty left over."

"Sorry," Riley replied, "but thanks for the offer."

She waited to lock the door before pulling the phone from her pocket. Two messages from Eugene:

Communion. One hour.

Bring your symbol.

Riley banged on the door as she yanked the lock open. "Mr. Crawford," she said.

The old man seemed puzzled for a moment.

"I'm really sorry, but I could I possibly borrow your car?"

The puzzled look continued.

"Messages," she said, flashing her phone fast enough that he wouldn't be able to see what it said. "It's not drink lids and stirring straws. I need to go, but the snow and everything . . ."

"Of course," he said, reaching into his pocket. "I won't need it until the morning so," he held the key out by the same compass key chain that was on hers. "Just be safe driving. Roads are damp."

"I will, Mr. Crawford. Thanks."

He waved one hand as he closed the door.

She locked the bolt. She heard its opposite do the same. The locks were an agreement that neither side could completely trust the other. It was how they could live in the same place together.

Of course, he also had a key for her front door. Someone had to be in charge.

Riley kept her hood up as she leaned against the wall to the left of the entrance into the 2Go Tesoro station. She watched as an older woman in a bright yellow snow jacket yanked the gas hose toward the tank she'd parked too far away. The only other car in the lot was Mr. Crawford's wood-paneled Datsun wagon that was probably twice her age yet started up and rode as well as such an old car can run through half an inch of snow.

She rubbed her gloved hands together in front

of her. She considered remaining in the car until Eugene showed, but doing so might make him think she wasn't there as he drove up. It was good timing for a communion, if only to keep from getting any colder.

The woman watched the meter of the gas pump. The nozzle popped repeatedly as she attempted to squeeze extra drops into her tank. Riley felt her hand doing the same: open and close, open and close. She imagined her own pop. The woman placed the hose back when a gray sedan pulled into a space two away from where Riley stood. The sedan was a generic one, like those auto dealers and rental places had in abundance, even down to a plain black license frame. She pushed off the wall. The headlights blacked out the car's interior. She opened the door.

Eugene was probably in his late thirties with thinning hair and a clean-shaven face. Neither of them spoke as the car pulled out of the lot and drove down the road. They'd spent almost a month in neighboring barracks underground but had only spoken three times before, and never during their first meeting: the night Riley saw her first wolf. The massive one, with sharp, knotty tufts like so many devil horns.

Twenty minutes of nothing but divider lines, reflectors, and snowflakes flying through the high beams. Eugene signaled once before turning toward a building that looked like a big box store that never opened. The car drove right up to the "reserved" parking spaces in front. No gate, no signs, nothing out front to look like anything more than a space awaiting someone to claim it. A sprinkling of snow covered a couple of cars occupying other reserved spaces. They weren't the same model as Eugene's—that would be suspicious—but they were just as nondescript.

Eugene's many keys jingled on the looping chain holding them all. He kneeled to unlock the bolt at the bottom of the door before opening the lock that kept the two sides of the entrance closed. Riley couldn't help wondering if the frosted glass of the door and windows would offer any defense at all. If she really wanted to, could she break in herself?

For a moment there was nothing but darkness inside. Riley blinked twice, held her eyes closed for a second, opened them. The room lit up.

Eugene locked the door behind them. Some snow had drifted in. The room reminded her of the Costco she'd once visited with her mom during a weeklong trip to Juneau, only the ceiling was about half as high to provide room for an upper floor. Doors near the back led to what she had assumed was a loading area as a pair of doors in the left corner hid a freight elevator large enough for anything from the Pointed Hand's complex to fit into, except for Virgil's stone slab of a desk. That might've been why he didn't bring it along.

Riley glanced back as she paced across the empty floor with its scuffs and scratches as though someone had played demolition derby with shopping carts. Eugene followed behind. Deep shadows covered his eyes as well.

"Quite a change from the old place," she said, as though trying to break the ice.

He didn't reply.

Riley checked out one of the large columns set about halfway from the entrance. Stray marks dotted between three and nine feet up its length. Riley imagined sparring partners kicking off the column during their matches. It had been a long time since she'd been tested in that way, not since facing off with a trio of recent recruits who hadn't taken to the blood nearly as well as she did. Some just weren't fit for this life. They were not chosen, as Virgil had said she was.

"Wolves have owned entire cities for centuries," Eugene said from over her shoulder. "We have only a few places of our own."

The elevator floor was nearly black with scrapes. Dents in the walls marked where posts had slammed into them. The door opened into one long hallway down the entire length of the building. Dove stood a few feet from the door. Her hands were folded in front of her and her long cloak draped to the floor like a stage curtain. Each tiny follicle of hair was clear on her scalp, while much of her face, from the brow to the top of her cheeks, was covered by the same inky black shade that covered Riley's own. They'd never seen each other eye to eye.

"I'll take her from here, Brother," Dove said calmly.

Eugene bowed as he reached to hold the elevator door open.

"He awaits you, Sister." The cloak whooshed as Dove turned away. "Do not disappoint."

Eugene exited the elevator behind Riley. He crossed his hands in front of him as he settled into a lean against the wall.

A series of three doors stretched down the wall to her left. Riley peeked into the first as she passed: a long barracks, divided in the middle for several bathrooms, with another barracks on the other side. The few men sitting at their desks, praying at the foot of their crucified cloaks, or napping on their beds told her that this was the men's side of the room. She'd have a bed reserved on the other side, if she were to be called in again. The second door was closed and locked. She'd previously seen it as a walk-in closet filled with wooden cases of weapons, the familiar blades, swords, daggers, pistols, and rifles she'd practiced with for almost two months underground. She never cared for the firearms. Too slow and unreliable. The blade strapped to her wrist caused a slight imbalance, but it was less restrictive of her movement than any of the other weapons.

Dove marched directly toward the last door in the hallway. She opened the door into another hall. "After you," she said, motioning for Riley to enter.

It was an updated version of those she'd seen under the barn: a series of closed doors with exactly matching handles down each side. She heard Dove's cloak swing gently behind her as she marched down the hallway. There were other sounds as well, a few stray people within the closed rooms, a slight hiss as she passed the third door on her right, which meant that garments were undergoing treatment inside. The hall ended in yet another door with the whir of a single gear within and a slight chill coming from underneath. She stopped at the last door on her right.

Dove stopped in place. She kept her hands low in front of her, one over the other, head up and shoulders back. The stance and long, formless cloak with the hood down made her look like a singer in a church choir. Riley knocked once on the door before opening.

Virgil wandered around the side of a desk that looked like something ordered from an office furniture catalog. "Sister Sapphira," he said. The strings tying together his collar were loose and his long, thinning hair was spread over his back. "Good to see your commitment remains solid." He motioned for Riley to enter.

She turned to pull the door closed just as Dove stepped in behind her. Riley stepped back. She furrowed her brow, staring into the deep darkness that covered Dove's eyes. That darkness seemed to stare back.

"What do you see?" Dove's voice was quiet, almost challenging.

"Sister Sapphira," Virgil called out from the other side of the room, "to business."

Dove cocked her head. "You have been summoned," she said, sliding away as she pulled the door closed. She resettled, hands folded in front of her, one step from the entrance, as though guarding against anything that might pass through it.

The shadowless room was as far from the previous one as possible: office chairs had replaced the old wooden ones and a metal and plastic rectangle took the place of the stone slab. There was a pair of doors along the left wall that led to a small bedroom in the front, and a smaller bathroom in the rear.

Only the armoire remained of the old place, pushed against the wall between the doors. Its intricate contours were an even greater contrast with the blank walls than they had been with the stonework.

"How's normal life treating you?"

"I'm acclimating," she replied.

"Making new friends?" he asked as he stepped to the front of the desk, between it and the now two chairs on the other side. It wasn't wide enough for three.

"Not really," she said.

"That's for the best." Virgil replied. "No need to get too close with people who will only be temporary."

Riley nodded.

"Temptations," he added. "We expect to lose some of our members to the comforts of this world. Yet those whose faith endures shall be rewarded."

Riley glanced toward the carved wooden doors of the armoire. Small, nearly undetectable dots of gray formed faint lines across and down the gaps between sides, leftover glue from the tape used to hold it shut. They'd replaced or left behind almost everything else: beds, chairs, desks, the empty barrels that smelled of old iron, even the portraits that lined the passage into the central chamber, yet this piece of antique storage remained.

"Yet faith has never driven you, has it, Sister?"

"I'm here," Riley said, "that should be worth something."

"Oh, it is, Sister. It's worth far more than you know."

He paced back around to the other side of the desk.

"I trust that you brought back what I requested."

"Yes, Father," she replied with a nod.

"Well, may I see it?"

Riley reached into her coat to pull out the Polaroid, now slightly curved from being kept pressed against her side. Virgil reached out to take it from her.

"This is how you were then," he said. "Disengaged. Apathetic."

"I didn't know any different," Riley replied.

"And your mother is there, holding you close while you seem disinterested."

Riley felt her shoulders begin to droop.

"She was a strong woman," Virgil said, "stoic, even as her heart shattered."

Riley remembered sitting on the bench in front of her apartment building on the day of the exodus. She stared at her mother's car, hoping for a turn toward her, a flash of a smile or a tear, anything, until the taillights disappeared into the mass of so many others.

"Curious you didn't choose a picture of your father."

"They're gone."

"Well then," Virgil replied. He reached out to her from the other side of the desk. "You are not this girl anymore. Directionless, wandering through a pitiful existence." He held the very edge of the photo flat, as though it floated above the ground. "You have a purpose."

"Yes, Father," Riley said again. She tucked the photo unseen back into her pocket.

"Very good."

Riley's eyes drifted toward Dove next to the door behind her.

"It seems your friend has become quite the celebrity."

"He isn't my friend," Riley snapped, eyes darting back to Virgil.

"Well," he started again, "the pup you once knew has been making television appearances. He's been drumming up sympathy for his kind."

"I haven't been watching much television lately," she lied. She'd seen every report from all over the country, the clash between soldiers and wolves in New Mexico, the protests outside of the fence in California, the lack of food in Illinois, the debates in Washington, and the tour of her former home, which made the whole city look like the isolated paradise it never was.

"You aren't the audience that concerns me, Sister," he followed up without question. "What concerns me are those who haven't witnessed the corruption as you and I have. Those who think evil can be mollified or reasoned with. It is this audience that should concern us."

"Hasn't that been our concern from the start?" she asked. "Protecting those who know nothing about the threat surrounding them?"

"Indeed it is, Sister, but as the threat has changed, so have we. It isn't merely enough to contain the corruption. It must be eradicated."

Her brow furrowed as she stared at him. Deep lines carved outward from the paleness of his eyes, exactly as they always had. The shadows covering Dove's eyes and those of Riley were absent from his face. They always had been.

"Shouldn't containment be enough?"

A tiny chuckle came from behind Riley.

"Has it ever been? Can you think of a single time when accepting an affliction has resulted in curing it?"

Riley's eyes lowered once more.

"The duty of the Hidden Blade, Sister, was

to watch, to disappear, to take action only when necessary."

Virgil pulled open a drawer within the desk.

"We are no longer hidden."

He reached into the drawer.

"It is the duty of the Pointed Hand to strike," Dove said from behind Riley.

Virgil placed a leather holster on the desk in front of him. Two pairs of straps trailed behind. Riley saw the silver and pearl handle of the revolver peeking out from the back of its cover.

"What's this about?" she asked.

"An excursion, like that which you undertook on your own." He removed his hand from the holster, leaving it on the edge of the desk. "Not tonight, but soon."

"But," Riley protested. "Our duty isn't to—"

"I've told you, Sister," Virgil snapped, "our duty has changed. The world has changed."

He paused a moment, calming himself.

"The Nobilitate Nobis was a temporary measure.

It was meant to delay the inevitable conflict as long as possible. But now, there is no more holding that conflict back." His eyes locked onto hers as though he were trying to read her thoughts. "This containment you speak of only allows the corruption to fester as it did in Enoch and Sodom. The creatures within that fence will become stronger, more potent, more dangerous, and eventually, they will get out."

"We aren't hunters," she said again.

A snicker came from Dove next to the door.

"I'm not asking you to hunt, Sister. I'm asking you to guard."

Riley tilted her head.

"There are certain documents which we require to prevent the Canaanites from corrupting more of the world outside of their fence. Documents which would bolster their claims of legitimacy."

"The town charter."

"Yes. Documented evidence of their right to exist in this place, according to the laws of Man."

"So?" Riley asked. "It sucks that I can't go home,

97

but at least the wolves aren't threatening anyone anymore."

"But that threat is growing every day, Sister," Virgil said. "Allowing them to stay legitimizes them in the eyes of the foolish. Legitimacy leads to demands of equality. And what happens when that equality isn't given? That's when the anger grows. The clashes, the fighting, the true battle. We've already seen its precursors in their settlements. Imagine that on a global scale, without even the chance of containment. Once that happens, there's no way to prevent its spread, the death, the destruction of all that remains pure in this world."

"And stealing the town charter will prevent that?" Riley questioned.

"No." Vigil's reply was two rocks smashing together. "But it deprives them of the legitimacy they seek. And it gives us a chance to prepare. Look at this place." He motioned to the rooms outside. "We're a shadow of our former selves. Our resources are paltry compared to those of our enemy."

Riley cocked her brow at this word.

"A quick foray into the heart of Wolfland, as you have demonstrated, enough to remove what we need from their possession."

Riley's eyes wandered around the room again.

"I'm not asking you to hunt anyone, Sister, but this is a dangerous trip, and you are the best among us, the favored of our Lord."

Riley's gaze steeled on him. She knew he wouldn't be able to see it. She glanced to Dove, her own stare hidden behind a matching shadow.

"I need you to be there, to watch as we walk amongst the corruption."

She felt her gaze soften.

"Our supplies are low. We have precious few of our previous resources, but you will receive every gift that has been bestowed upon us." He picked the holster up from the desk. "All we have and more," he said as he approached her. "Not every soldier is worthy. Some paths lead only to sacrifice." He came to a stop directly in front of her. The pistol in his hand lingered just under her eye line. "You, Sister Sapphira, are not only worthy, you are chosen."

He held the holster out to her. The belt straps were folded under its weight.

"I know," she said.

"More than you know. More than anyone else."

Riley glanced quickly over her shoulder once more. Dove remained unmoved; what Riley could see of her wore no expression. The good soldier, following, never doubting.

"You have been chosen to lead us, after I fall," he said.

"You expect to die during this excursion?" Riley asked, looking past his extended arm.

"No," he said, shoving the pistol toward her, its handle pointing as though begging her to take it. "I will not fall that day. But when my time comes, I want you to use this."

He rotated his hand to drop the holster. Riley instinctively caught it. It was heavier than she expected and yet not heavy at all.

"Our mission must continue, Sister, until the corruption is stricken."

She looked down at the object in her hand. The leather was worn to a near polish. The metal shined as one solid piece of silvery steel. Its pearl handle was decorated with swirls and spirals patterned like wood grain, as though carved into the flat sides.

He nodded for her to remove the pistol.

The metal was cold and uncompromising. She saw the outline of her distorted reflection in the grooves of the bullet chamber. The hammer curved up and out like the sliver of a crescent moon. Shapes along the barrel caught her eyes. She leaned closer. Words were carved long the length of metal.

And he that curseth his father or his mother shall surely be put to death.

"Come, sister," Virgil's voice pulled her back into the room. "What remains of our sacramental wine is yours."

CHAPTER 6

"CLEAN CUT, JUST LIKE THE LAST ONE," THE young man kept his head down as he spoke. He brushed his sandy hair from his eyes. He was maybe fifteen or sixteen years old. Nate hadn't seen many people in town who were younger than he was. He must have had his Feral Right at twelve or thirteen, when most of them do. "Nothing else. No scents, no tracks."

There were younger children as well, a couple of babies and elementary school kids. They obviously hadn't changed yet. They probably would though. Their parents had.

"Are you confident that it wasn't the Order?" Ulrich asked the boy.

"Not confident, High Councilor."

There had been a debate about whether non-wolf spouses or children from such mixed couples, who hadn't yet demonstrated a predilection toward changing, should remain or be exiled.

"The Order wouldn't cut the fence," Maier answered. "Any blackrobe would know better than to leave evidence. Especially not twice in a few days."

Eventually the question to stay or leave was answered when the fence went up, and the food and power went down. Those who could leave, left. No one else had a choice.

"Cover their tracks," Zarker growled, one fang peeking from under his curled lip.

"Maybe," replied Maier, "but obviously there's little we can do to stop intruders."

Zarker snorted one frustrated breath.

"Shouldn't the soldiers see this?" Clarkson offered to the group.

"Not their concern," Maier retorted. "The Guard isn't there to keep others out. Neither is the fence."

"That's why it's imperative that we continue to self-regulate," Ulrich added. "If we can demonstrate an ability to keep peace among ourselves, and not become reactionary or paranoid, then we'll show those outside of the fence that we are civilized rather than wild."

Zarker snorted once more. Several others nodded.

"We should do so regardless of what the outsiders think," Maier added as a variation of Ulrich's statement. Fewer nods followed.

Nate surveyed the people gathered in the center of the museum floor. Ulrich faced the door again, under the head of the blue whale hanging from the ceiling. Shayera stood, as always, one step behind his side. A few others separated her from Clarkson, a few more before the sandy-haired boy who kept his head down as he spoke. Nate and his mother stood just off from opposite to Ulrich. Zarker stood a couple of steps back from the rest of the gathered circle with Maier as nine o'clock to Ulrich's twelve. Word of a second hole in one week spread quickly, as did the delay in supplies. There were forty, maybe fifty, other members filling the spaces between the ones Nate knew well. The crowd pushed outward and broke around the octagonal information display under the whale. Nate still didn't know all of these people, but they knew him. That was certain. Some, he imagined, might've used their concern as an excuse just to watch the proceedings. It was something to do other than sit around pining after some fabled time before.

Ulrich continued, "If we can remain peaceful, follow the plan we agreed to, then within the next year we may be able to garner enough public sympathy to force the authorities to grant us basic rights and amenities."

Most were in their human forms while Zarker and half a dozen others stood among them as wolves. Two of them wore robes, one with little yellow daisies patterned along the front. Nate had to keep himself from chuckling when he had walked in to find a stocky wolf with deep red eyes, and short, pinned-back ears like a pair of horns, dressed in bright flowers.

"We have a long-standing claim to this town," Ulrich continued. "We must use that."

"All due respect, High Councilor," Maier said, his tone fitting such a remark, "while our long-term goal may remain restoration of the city, it would perhaps be more beneficial for all of us, those inside and outside of the fence, if we give special attention to what we can do to strengthen ourselves."

Nate noted the looks of agreement on several of those gathered. He glanced to his mother. Her face was stern, expressionless.

"Our ancestors lived without luxuries. Surely we can do the same."

"Councilor," Ulrich replied, "as you have stated before, our ancestors did not face the same perils as we do now. Especially since our presence has become so well known."

"How will we know what the public thinks?" asked Sobetsky, one of the councilors whom Nate wasn't familiar with.

"Our Ambassador will tell us," Ulrich said. His tone was drenched in mockery. A few of those near him snorted, others scowled.

The boy looked up along with dozens of eyes shifting in Nate's direction. His expression was one of sudden surprise, almost disbelief. The others were less impressed. Nate's mother didn't look away from Ulrich.

All were welcome to attend the meetings but not all were *welcome* to speak.

Ulrich turned toward the boy, who continued staring wide-eyed at Nate. "Thank you for your report, Clint."

"Yes, High Councilor," the boy said with a sudden, jolting nod. The crowd parted to let him through. He wandered toward the back where a very tall man placed his hand on the boy's shoulder. The boy's eyes found Nate once again, wide as though starstruck. Nate looked across the circle to where Ulrich remained a step in front of everyone else.

Ulrich shrugged his shoulders in practiced annoyance. "I suppose we will have to initiate yet another count, Ambassador Wallace," he said. A look of distain caught Nate's view. "What was the result of the previous count?"

"Two hundred sixty-eight," he said, meeting Ulrich's displeasure with his own.

"And how many were there for the count the soldiers requested last week?"

"Two hundred sixty-eight."

"How many do you expect that number will be after the soldiers' inevitable request for yet another count following this last breach?"

Nate felt the distaste on his face as he stared across the gap in the circle of onlookers.

"Perhaps the less predictable question is whether you will fulfill your assigned duty this time," Ulrich asked after Nate's silence, "or will you once again abandon your responsibilities?"

Nate's burning stare shifted briefly to Shayera before returning to Ulrich.

"I will happily take this responsibility, High Councilor," Nate said with as much sincerity as could break through his distain. "In fact, I don't understand why you seem to think so little of the counts when they demonstrate the exact type of cooperation with the Guard that you constantly advocate."

"Cooperation is a good thing, Ambassador," Ulrich replied, exactly as Nate expected, even down to the ironic title, "but these repeated gatherings only to learn nothing new are becoming a too frequent interruption in our daily lives."

"You call them interruptions, but you don't even attend them yourself," Nate replied. There were snickers in the crowd.

"The Council has more important matters to

discuss than counting the same number over and over again."

"It might be the same number but at least it's something to do."

Nate heard stifled laughter mixed with disapproving grunts.

"Does anyone here remember what they did on Monday?" Nate glanced at the puzzled looks surrounding him. "Or the day before that? Other than attend another council meeting." His mother chuckled lightly. "But I bet most people remember everything about the day we last received supplies. I bet most people remember when we took our last count two days ago." He motioned across the circle. "I remember Lady Shayera and I leaving this meeting to find Mr. Zarker and Mr. Barber, so that we could gather our entire population together in one place." He paused for a second before adding, "You know, there's only two hundred sixty-eight people in this whole town, and we still aren't familiar enough with each other to know who, if anyone, is missing."

"A reality that never could have come to pass if not for your actions," Ulrich remarked.

Nate's mother growled quietly.

"You think I don't know that? You and probably half of everyone else in this room remind me of it every day." He glanced toward Shayera, who looked quickly away. "And it's not like I was ever going to forget. But this is our reality now—being stuck in here, with so few of us, with no power, little food, and nothing else. And that's my point, High Councilor. People are bored."

He heard light chuckles from the rear of the crowd, those far enough back to not be seen.

"Supply drops, counts, even these meetings, they're something to do."

He felt the eyes around him were looking at him with interest rather than judgment.

"I used to fill my days with movies. Sitting with friends, talking about meaningless things we all agreed on and had talked about a thousand times before. But it was a way to pass the time while waiting for more important things to happen." He exhaled his own laugh. "One could say the same thing about these meetings."

There were snickers in the crowd.

"We come here every day so that the members of this council may repeat the same positions they've been stating for months." Sounds of disapproval overtook those of amusement. "And that's great," Nate added to his own disbelief.

Ulrich squinted at him as though suspicious.

"In fact, I propose that for the time being we open these meetings even more." Nate looked from Ulrich's face to the faces of those he didn't know. "Not just to attendance but"—he struggled to think of a fancy parallel—"for people to talk."

There were murmurs among the crowd.

"It's a break from tradition, but so is this entire situation. We're in unexplored territory, and it's time we try something new. And if nothing else, it's something to do. I mean, I've attended dozens of these meetings myself, and it's not like most of them are any different. It's mostly just you"—he motioned toward Ulrich—"telling us how we need to stay with the plan we 'all agreed on.'"

A laugh seemed to catch in Maier's throat.

"Or you"—Nate motioned toward Maier—"talking about ancestors and this mythological time before human interference when wolves were free to do whatever we wanted, which, if it was anything like now, was sit around and be bored." Maier raised his chin in Nate's direction. "When we aren't complaining about the lack of food or water or electricity, so that we can do anything other than nothing," Nate added.

"You're bored?" Ulrich scoffed. "We're talking about our very survival in a world that fears and hates our kind, and you want to complain that you're bored?"

Nate struggled for a moment as attention again shifted to him. "I mean . . . aren't you? Isn't that why we're here in this room talking about the exact same things every single day? If you haven't convinced us of your plan by now, you probably never will."

"So what would you propose?" Ulrich said, sticking his chin out so the white hair of his beard became a cliff.

"Jobs," Nate replied.

Ulrich snorted a laugh, others did as well.

"We need people to monitor the fence. Let's organize volunteer patrols ourselves. We could have two or three people go out to different sections a couple of times every day, rotate between different groups, like we do with the shack next to the inner gate or the cleanup crews, or the people who remove the snow from the parking lot, even though no one has a car."

Maier tilted his head in interest. Some lining the circle nodded.

"People would have to go out as humans, of course, but it's not that hard to get there. A few hours out of the day when there's nothing else to do. It would even show the soldiers that we're respecting their boundary. That we can govern ourselves. It demonstrates our cooperation. As you always say."

Ulrich leaned back as though attempting to withdraw from the conversation.

"The soldiers are bored too, and they hate the cold. Maybe if we show how peaceful we are, then there'll be less incentive for them to stay." Nate glanced over to Maier, arms folded over his chest. "We'll be left alone. Like you always talk about." Maier nodded. "Having patrols might stop whoever keeps cutting the fence. We're probably being watched by the drones, or the Order, or whoever else. Having a few people out there could hold them back. We could even have backup in the tree line," Nate replied. "A few people watching just in case. It doesn't take more than a few seconds to sprint from the trees to the fence if needed."

"What about those who can't walk the fence?" asked another member of the group, someone Nate didn't remember ever hearing before. "Or who won't?"

"There could be other jobs as well. We should have some way of knowing how many people are here without having to round everyone up for a count."

"A census," offered Clarkson.

"And then if someone does go missing, we'll know exactly who it is," Nate continued. "We're not that big of a town. We don't have to know everybody, but we should at least know someone who connects us to everyone else. Like Six Degrees of Kevin Bacon."

There were looks of confusion.

"It's a game," Nate said. "There could be other jobs too. More cleanup crews, people to take stock of what's salvaged during cleanup, people to come up with ideas on better water distribution, projects, stuff that happens in a real city." He raised a hand in Ulrich's direction. Ulrich glared at him. "You want things to go back to how they were. This is a step towards that. Instead of talking endlessly about one thing that we're waiting to do, let's allow people to actually do stuff. The Council doesn't need to manage everything."

"They want in," Zarker snarled, "they get in. Fence not enough. Patrol not enough." Every syllable was as sharp as the fur covering his back and shoulders. "Need to know to keep out." His long head bobbed up and down. "Anyone watch, I show them to be afraid. Show them to keep out."

"We can't appear hostile," Nate said.

Zarker snarled.

"But I'm sure anyone who saw you would run."

Zarker seemed to smile.

"I'd take a walk along the fence a couple of times a week," said Clarkson, nodding toward Nate. "If only to have something to do."

"I can help with patrols," said another man who stood two rows back from the circle. Nate craned to see him. He noticed Mrs. Wald standing at the man's side.

A woman raised her hand. "Nothing better to do," she added.

"I'll take a shift as well," Nate's mom said from his side. "I think we all should. It'll help keep us safer and more active." She paused for a moment before continuing. "And it's a way of getting more people involved with our community. It'll help us trust each other."

"I'll join the patrol as well," added Maier.

Zarker snorted before nodding.

Another hand went up. Nate noticed Ulrich looking over to the man as he did the same. The man looked only at Nate. "Yes?"

"I can help patrol, too," the man said as though uncertain about speaking. "But you mentioned water distribution. I know we have some pipe left over from a few of the buildings. I think if we move water from the stream in and out of the fountain, we could keep it from freezing. Maybe add a few rocks for friction." He looked around the room as though seeking confirmation. "I mean it still wouldn't be as clean as we're used to, but it'd be an easy supply for the older people. It'll probably overflow, but we wouldn't have to wait for supply shipments all the time."

The man looked to the others and then back to Nate. Eyes landed on him.

"It's worth trying," he said, nodding.

A woman leaned forward from the crowd around Maier.

"I've been wanting to help with the cleanup but never gotta say anything."

"I'm not sure who does cleanup," Nate replied, "but I'm sure whoever it is would be happy to have more people. Or just, you know, take a few others and do it yourself. You can't exactly steal anything," he said with a laugh.

Others among the group nodded.

Another among the group stepped up to volunteer.

Then another.

And another.

By the end, more people had spoken than hadn't.

Ulrich left immediately after declaring the meeting over. Shayera followed a few steps behind. Maier slapped Nate on the back as he walked past. Zarker nodded. Clarkson put his hand out to shake. "Good job," he said before moving on. Others did the same.

Nate's mother waited near the entrance as the afternoon's attendees exited the room. She nodded goodbye to them, watching as they passed. A few stragglers remained behind, talking among themselves.

"You're like him," she said while Nate paced toward the door.

"Who?" Nate said as he stepped out of the gallery.

She pointed toward the name on the wall.

"He wasn't as reactionary or—" She shook her

head, stopping herself. "Anyway, did you know he didn't ask to be a Councilor?"

Nate gave her a puzzled look as they walked through the lobby.

"Yeah, he just wanted to help. Eventually they figured out he'd keep trying to help whether they wanted him to or not, so they may as well bring him into their group."

She placed her hand on his shoulder as they stepped out of the open doorway.

"I'm sorry," she said. "I really am."

"It's okay, Mom." The snow was nearly blinding in the daylight. The whole city seemed to shine. "I understand."

CHAPTER 7

S TEAM.

Thin and white. Streaming from the street as though the snow itself were melting so quickly that it rose into the air as clouds that swirled into dozens of tiny storms. It parted as he moved, the rising trails pushing back even the buildings themselves, as though they, too, were made of the same melting white that covered the ground beneath his shoes. Above, in the black of the sky, the stars spiraled into millions of distant universes, light defining their shape in the way the dark outlined the twisted, steamy storms all around.

Nate saw small patches of growth beneath the blanket ahead. Little sprouts, the tops of carrots and tomato plants, frozen solid and steaming. He reached to touch the tomato leaves, the backs of his hands bare and clean. The leaf crumbled upon contact. A shake ran through the stem. It shattered. The entire plant broke into millions of tiny flakes that fell into the blank white. The plant blended to invisible as though it had never existed. He placed his fingers on the ground. Steam rose around them as though hot metal had been plunged into cold water.

"None may stray," he heard whispered into his ear.

He looked up. In front of him a circle of people replaced the melting shapes of buildings. They pulsed and swirled as storm clouds. Their heads reached into the sky, blanking out the stars themselves.

"None may stray," he heard the chorus thunder upon him.

He sensed something on his left shoulder. The

spot where Dove's blade had pierced his skin. He turned to a familiar face of pale skin and dark eyes, a square chin, and a streak of blond hair in black.

"Our world," said Riley.

She slid around him across the steaming floor. The crowd in the distance smoldered in towers of white and gray clouds.

"I hope I never see you again," Riley said, smiling. Her eyes drifted downward. Her hands rose. Strands of brown and black hair flowed from the back of her forearms, as long and dark as that on her head. Sharpened glass topped each of her fingers into extended claws. "I thought you were human," she said.

Another face appeared where Riley had been. Shayera stared directly into his eyes. A black swirl rose from her pupils. It gathered and formed into a shape over her forehead: the Eye of Providence. Shadows steamed off her toned shoulders and arms. "We're still hiding," she said.

Riley, on his other side, said, "I hope I never see you again."

"The rest of us would have to suffer," said Shayera. "Again."

The billowing crowd had grown thicker and darker, the storm within them growing. Cliff walls surrounded him.

"I hope I never see you again."

"None may stray," said Shayera. She lifted her hands in front of her. A pair of blades popped from the back of her forearms.

"I hope I never see you again."

"Still hiding," Shayera said, her arms lowering. "Have to suffer."

A black ash gathered over the blades. It covered the world around him. The light layer of snow was replaced by a thick layer of ash.

"I see you," Riley said. "I never hope again."

The walls began to shake and shatter. An avalanche of black smoke blasted toward him. Both Shayera and Riley lowered their hands. The ash ate through Shayera's blades. The glass shattered from Riley's fingers. The ash hit them from behind like a tidal wave.

Nate felt the smoke reaching into his nose as tendrils. It dug through his mouth and eyes, the pores of his skin. It coated his tongue and teeth and down the back of his throat. It burned, like the heat when changing. He could smell the smoke filling his lungs. He coughed. Ash streamed like cold breaths. He coughed again. Heavy hacks came from deep inside. Plumes of black smoke puffed out. He coughed and coughed.

He opened his eyes to darkness. Shapes emerged quickly: a pair of jeans folded over the top of an opened box on top of another box, the bare wall of his new room, clothes on the floor, the remaining boxes.

He sniffed at the air. He sensed a trace of something he couldn't quite identify. He inhaled sharply. Burning. Nate yanked a wadded-up sweatshirt from the floor. He pulled it on as he opened the door into the small living room of the new apartment.

A distinct odor of smoke greeted him outside, so thick it seemed to overwhelm him even as a human. The room was empty. His mother's door was open. The front door was as well. Heavy footsteps bounded through the hallway. He followed them out.

"The hell's going on?" he asked the first person he saw, a heavy-set woman in a thick robe who stood looking down from the top of the second floor staircase. She looked back at him with big eyes of equal parts shock and hesitation. She stepped back as Nate rushed forward, down the stairs, and continued toward the trio of people gathered inside the open front door. The smell of smoke filled the lobby of the apartment building.

Halloween orange framed the buildings across the road. The firelight flickered along the street and disappeared behind them. Several pillars of black smoke carved paths through the drifting snow. His mother stood off the curb ahead. The glow cut a line through the town. The smoke clouds appeared smaller, newer the farther they moved in, leading through the city from the western side. Then the line of fires stopped three blocks away. The plaza. No. The museum.

Others gathered on the curb around him. He saw the panic on their faces, heard the confusion in their voices. He pushed toward his mother. She glanced at him as he stepped down from the curb. He stared straight ahead. An orange glow framed black shadows. Obviously a fire. Several of them. He could nearly hear the crackle, feel the heat, taste the smoke. Even now, distant and dulled, the picture was clear. He felt himself shake.

"Nate," he heard his mother say.

The sides of his mouth twitched. He tasted copper on his tongue. His bones burned.

"Stay here," he said, the words streaming out of his mouth in one sustained sound.

She shook her head. "Don't—"

"Keep them safe." He tossed one hand toward the people on the sidewalk behind him.

He felt the heat growing both inside and out as he started running. He pushed through the shaking in his bones. Hair emerged from his skin. He felt each strand as a quick shot of piercing pain. The clothing burst and flew from his body. He tossed off the shreds. His teeth pressed together as top and bottom pushed from within his mouth. He felt the power growing in every step, striding farther until his motion changed from running on two legs to bounding on all four. The world went from fiery glow and black smoke and shadows to an explosion of burning light and swirling dark. The smoke was a dense, impenetrable black. The fire was bright red and yellow and orange. Both were everywhere. He raced toward the light.

Vague shapes peeked between gaps in the clouds of scent. It was like driving through a thick fog. Only he couldn't go slow. He had to speed. As he had that first night.

The crackle of the fires grew as he approached. Then came the scrapes and growls—guttural and vicious—screams and yelps, all in pain. New scents appeared beneath and between the holes of heat and burning: singed hair and blood. They clustered in little pockets along the road to the plaza grounds. Fires tracked from the outside of the town. It was hard to tell exactly where they came from. Their scents flowed everywhere. Might be easier if he could see—actually see—but then he'd be slower, weaker, less ready for what might come. Heat from the fires grew as he rushed on. The orange glow intensified. Nearly blinding, as it was meant to be. The smoke was black clouds suffocating a bright field. Everything else seemed to be ghosts. He heard a sharp yowl cut through it all. Then a wet choke. He ran toward the sound.

Crowds of specters fought each other. The vague shapes of long creatures bent forward as they swung at smaller shapes, some of them scattered points like constellations, groups of them, more of the small than the large. They drifted through the cloudy orange like a distant army. Impossible to tell how many, how close, or how they moved, or if they were even there at all.

A gunshot echoed off the buildings to one side of the street. Nate crouched low to the ground. The vapor of melting snow drifted up, as did the smoke, leaving thin mist near his feet. One last street between him and the south entrance of the plaza. He stayed low as he approached. He slowed, as though stalking, absorbing as much of the scene as possible. Distant figures continued to spin and strike at each other. Those closer, those he could see between the cold and the heat, were still. He placed his hand out as he approached one. Metallic streams leaked from it, a male. Small holes punctured his chest, one through his neck. A thick patch of blood ran from its throat, already still and cooling. It was human, wearing nothing but an oversized robe. Nate tuned in for a heartbeat. There was none. The others were silent as well, all of them human, some clothed and some not, some stabbed and slashed, some ripped and gutted, strewn across the road and into the center park like a trail. A trail leading . . .

A sharp growl followed a loud scream. One large figure turned to leap at a smaller, dotted form. The wolf was clear to him as vague shapes encroached from behind. Nate sprinted on. Patterns in the others grew denser as he approached. Their scents were more active than those of the fire or the smoke. The outlines hinted at long cloaks with pointed arms moving to surround the larger form that twisted around itself as though uncertain where to face next. It stopped. The bright orange of the fires behind made the figure little more than a blurred silhouette in Nate's mind. Those around it hopped back and forth as though dancing. The one in the center, the wolf, charged to strike at one. It shifted back impossibly quick. Two others jumped in. Nate heard a pair of wet slices. A howl. They jumped back as the wolf reeled to swing. Nate charged. He leapt at one of the attackers.

He roared upon landing. He felt the bones break in the body beneath him. He swung one massive hand downward. A spray of blood followed. He felt it stick to his fingers as he struck again. He felt his claws shred skin. The body kicked beneath his weight. He sensed moisture from the figure's eyes. Panic surged through his blood. Nate sliced two fingers across the blackrobe's throat.

Another nearby invader, and another behind that one, backed away. Nate growled at them. They were constellations shivering in firelight. He jumped, swinging blindly. Fabric ripped with some flesh. He heard what sounded like words, but couldn't make out the words themselves. His second swing pulled against his fingers. His claws caught before cutting.

They are people, he thought, as though a tiny voice were whispering into the back of his mind. He could have known them. Classmates. Friends. He shook his head. He smelled his own adrenaline rushing through his body. He growled as the other blackrobe retreated. He was a set of disconnected oval spots, a poor palm print stamped over the fire with smoke clouds still drifting between them.

They are people, he thought again. *And so are we.*

A blur took the blackrobe down. Sharp edges of dirt and grease barely emerged through the smoke and heat. The wolf buried its teeth into the fallen attacker's throat. Several other shadows drew nearer. Several more remained in the distance.

"Shayera," Zarker growled. "Museum." He rose up as though uncurling himself. He burned as much as the fires. "Help her."

Zarker lurched forward, contracting into a dense set of points, like the head of a morning star. He roared as he faded into the light. There was pleasure in his battle cry. Nate followed. He felt the snow spray from the kick of his legs. He felt the thick coat of blood over his fingers. It nipped at his nose even under the dense walls of smoke and fire. They were people. *Were.* Not anymore.

Nate sprinted on. Shadows rose and fell around him. The orange began to fade as the snow started suppressing the fires. The smoke was a haze, a dust filter over a camera lens. The figures started to become clear with fewer dense clouds to hide behind. Whatever they'd used to make themselves invisible before seemed to lessen as well.

A pair of blackrobes came into view straight ahead. Their backs were to him, facing toward another wolf. Nate charged one of them. There was an impact at his forearm and a loud crunch of bone. The blackrobe flew as though hit by a speeding car. The wolf pounced upon the other. Nate didn't break his stride.

A skirmish blocked the path from the plaza to the museum lot. Nate veered to leap over the fence and onto the light snow fallen on the asphalt. He didn't slow. He charged up the stairs toward where old stone and metal outlined the museum entrance. Drifts of dead skin and blood passed by. A body lay on the second landing up the stairs, naked, one of his. Another lay near the top, a female wolf on its stomach. One hand still stretched outward. He sensed the hole through her chest and a clean slice across her belly. An old scent on it, dander caked on overlapping skin. A blood trail streaked up the stairs. She'd dragged herself up in a desperate effort to stop the intruders.

Nate heard an extremely faint heartbeat as he approached. She was thin, almost frail. Too small to be Shayera. The scent of coffee grew as he neared. Annabelle Moore.

He placed his hand gently against the thinning, gray fur on her back. Her breath leaked out, so weak it seemed any pressure might suffocate her. Blood pooled under her stomach and chest, soaking through the hair and up to the skin. She'd never heal in time to stop it.

He lowered his head toward hers. Her breath fluttered the longer hairs on the side of his jaw. Her hand lifted from the pavement and he placed his hand over the back of hers. Her head lowered to the ground as she let out one, long breath. Her heartbeat faded.

The field beyond was a wasteland of drifting smoke and fire. He saw the veiled shapes of his kind engaged with them. Wolves circled as though surrounding. Growls and grunts and screams and roars. They fought ghosts and stars. Blood sprayed over the snow. Bodies, all of them human, lay bloodied and still. The vaguely familiar scent of Zarker was still out there. Seemed to be others as well. People he knew, from now or from before. Perhaps not their names, perhaps not even their faces, but at some point in time they had shared the same space. And they did again now. Nothing more familiar than that. Not that he could see anything through whatever the blackrobes used to cloak themselves, the haze and clouds that stung the inside of his nose. He took one last look.

Maybe Riley had left after all. He ran for the museum doors.

Shayera was crouched in front of the entrance to the main gallery. The traces of smoke and fire in the room trailed off Shayera and those she'd followed before stopping here, hiding behind the gallery entrance. Spots of dampness lined the lobby. Dirt and grease wafted from the carpet, which hadn't been cleaned since the exodus. Beyond the wall were exhibits, panes of glass containing old paint and bones and mildew. Coffee lingered around the reception desk where Annabelle Moore always sat.

"They have him," Nate heard as a whisper nearby. Shayera kept her hand on one of the doors as she leaned toward him. "Ulrich."

Nate crawled closer. "How many?"

She shook her head.

In the center of the front gallery was one small spot, bright as the sun, washing out the space immediately around it. Virgil would have others with him, or at least one, cloaked better than those outside. Outside were the cannon fodder, he'd have the elite. Nate took a deep breath through his nose, the scents rushed into his mind. The bright spot concentrated into a central point. The Eye of Providence looked back at him.

Nate felt the heat beginning to rise inside himself again. His nose contracted with a low growl. Shayera put one finger up to him. Probably the closest either of them could get to saying, "Shhh."

He positioned himself on the other side of the closed entrance. He leaned closer. He focused on the sound. Those inside whispered. Feet tapped the floor, many of them. A muffled metallic echo stepped in syncopated rhythm.

Of course, Dove would be there. She was everywhere. The growl started again.

"No."

Nate glanced across at Shayera.

"Could hurt the High Councilor."

Nate stared at her. His mouth pulled back. His teeth showed. The claws surged pain through each of his fingertips. His veins were laced with fire.

"Not yet."

She held one palm out to him, claws withdrawn. It was red in his mind.

"Wait," she said. "Wait."

Nate squeezed his eyes shut. His chest heaved with seethed breath. He focused on the sounds beyond the wall, imagined pulling into them like a camera zoom. They were moving away, toward the rear of the gallery. There was a scraping sound among the steps, something or someone being dragged along. The taps were too many and too irregular to trace. There remained the scents of smoke and fire, but twisted, thin and spotty. A pause in the steps. A metal creak. Some words he couldn't hear. A slam loud enough that he didn't have to concentrate on it.

"Now," Shayera said, "follow. Quiet."

Shayera placed her entire forearm over the push bar of the door. The metal inside scraped quietly as she slowly applied pressure. One louder click as the latch moved. She froze. Nate did as well.

No sound from inside.

She held the door. Blood surged through her fingertips as long claws emerged.

"They will see," she said, a rumble to her tone. "Hard fight. Be quick."

Nate growled through his teeth.

"Ready?"

CHAPTER 8

*I*T WASN'T SUPPOSED TO BE LIKE THIS.

Riley's thoughts rang through her mind as though yelled in from an outside voice.

It wasn't supposed to be like this.

Flames licked from the sporting goods store on the corner. Or what used to be a sporting goods store. She couldn't remember the name exactly, but back in grade school she had purchased a pair of running shoes there for PE class. Now smoke billowed out in one massive cloud stretching from the burning window boards to as high as she could see.

Cold metal pressed against her hip. She shifted

slightly to let the pistol sit more comfortably at her side. She was supposed to be there as support. She was supposed to be there to watch and possibly back up. This was a quick run into the town. A heist. She was Linus to Virgil's Danny Ocean—the remake version. They were supposed to slip in and out undetected, as she had done before. Virgil had never said anything about lighting fires on their way in, drawing the entire town's attention, or using the heat and smoke to cover their movements through the town and into the museum, or having dozens of her fellow guardians rush into the town center like an invading army.

It wasn't supposed to be like this.

The fire was a flicker over the plain white snow, which fell indifferently upon all those under it. She looked to the plaza grounds across the road. The smoke shifted from a dense black to a transparent gray. She still saw it stream outward. The haze filled the entire area. She saw through it as she did shadows and darkness, even trees and the cloaks of her brothers and sisters. Her senses made the patterns in her mind. She saw the chaos in detail, the way her brothers' cloaks moved as they hopped back from a savage swipe, the wolf's short, dense hairs waving from motion, the tension in the fist that plunged a blade into the surrounded wolf's back. The blade emerged bloody. It sprayed red across the light snow covering the path toward the fountain at the center of the plaza. The wolf spun at the second attacker. She saw this fight repeated all over the field in front of her. The cloaks outnumbered the furs, maybe three to one. The furs outsized the cloaks by about the same, one to three.

A trail of bodies led from the gate into the plaza grounds. Some were cloaked, some were naked—all were dead. All were flesh and bone and bleeding and still. She could taste their blood coated on her tongue and teeth.

Patches of snow bore dozens of shades from red to light pink. The wolf ahead of her seemed to swing wildly. If she could smell the smoke filling the town, then they—the wolves, the Canaanites, the corrupted—must be overwhelmed by it. The closest wolf, brown with a pair of black spots, took a long swipe at one of the two cloaks surrounding it. The brother dodged easily. The other seized the opportunity to strike, plunging a sword through its back and out of its chest. The wolf roared as it crumbled to one knee, then to its hands, then to the ground. The two cloaks jumped in, stabbing the wolf repeatedly. One of the two pointed into the distance, to the other side of the plaza fountain. A pair of wolves faced off against a trio of their brothers. He took off as the other wiped his sword across the glove over his hand. He licked the blood up before following the first.

They were supposed to be guardians.

A scream cut through the noise. It stopped rather than faded. Riley watched as a dark blur streaked toward the center of the field ahead. The wolf moved so fast she could barely make out its size or shape. It smashed into the second of the two cloaks dashing down the path. The man broke in half against the rim around the fountain. The wolf slashed with mad, wild strikes before running after the remaining of the two brothers she'd watch kill the wolf by the gate.

A pistol fired. A blunderbuss exploded. Riley squinted to see the darting wolf meet another on the far side of the fountain. It leapt into one of the cloaks surrounding its fellow. The other brothers immediately shifted away. The fallen brother screamed as a flurry of strikes ripped him apart. The wolf continued to tear. Dark points of matted fur came into focus on the wolf's shoulders and back. She could see the panic in the three cloaks who remained. They still had the numbers, but that number was shrinking by the second while the wolves, however many were yet to join the fight, remained large.

Two more dark shapes entered the south side of the plaza. They immediately dashed into the fight. More could still come. Her people, as they were, would be overwhelmed. They were already short-handed, short supplied. The Order was already compromised, a shadow of its former self. The fires were dying from the falling snow. Wind had begun dissipating the smoke. Virgil said they had little of their supplies left. All they had were numbers, and those were quickly falling. Without the cover of the smoke and the fire, they'd be exposed. They'd be slaughtered. The big wolf slashed two of the cloaks down with one swipe. The other wolf took care of the last. They *were* being slaughtered.

She was supposed to be backup. She might be all they had.

The berserking wolf launched toward another pair of humans standing over a still-changed body on the path leading away from the museum. One fired a pistol. The other swung his sword. The first lost his hand. The other lost his head. The wolf turned again as though stalking for his next kill.

Fighting continued in pockets along the outer reaches of the plaza while the wild-haired wolf patrolled the center. He marched cautiously as though struggling to see through the smoke lingering in the air. The smoke would only grow thinner. His hunt would continue.

It wasn't supposed to be like this, she thought again. *But it is.*

The snow crunched under her feet as she sprinted toward a fight at the edge of the plaza. Snowflakes fluttered over her head as she ran. She squeezed her fingers tightly. There was a howl as the blade cut through the air.

One wolf swung at a pair of men. Its claws moved in long, flailing swipes that never seemed to end. There was no hesitation in its motion. A frenzied beast going for the kill. They had no choice but to put it down.

Riley angled to catch the beast between herself and the others. She kicked out one leg as she neared, dropping into a baseball slide across the snow. She carved her blade up the back of the wolf's leg. It howled in pain. She popped up to her feet, withdrew her blade, and continued running. There was a short yelp as the others finished off the injured. She didn't have to kill them, but she couldn't let them kill. She raced on.

The large one stalked across the ground in front of her. She saw the shake in the thin points sticking out of its fur. Dried blood caked its clenched teeth and the long claws that encrusted its hands. She recognized the angled strands on its forearms, the savageness in the way it moved, with spit dripping from its lips. Its red eyes passed over her, just as it had the night when she saw her first wolf in the flesh, so to speak. It had been this one.

She moved in an erratic, serpentine motion toward it. Its low stance with stretched-out arms and extended claws made it appear the width of a car. Even lowered like this, it would still tower over her. She skirted around the edge of where the four paths joined in the center of the plaza. The haze of smoke remained as a layer over her vision. She kept watching as she circled around. Fights continued in every corner of the plaza, the symmetrical quadrants. The smoke must still be working. Her clothes had been treated as well. She checked the metal cuff over the back of her hand. Blood dotted where she'd withdrawn the blade. She'd have the advantage, but not for long. The scent of the blood on her hand and on her blade would quickly give her away. She waved around the benches and snow-covered shrubs in the center of the plaza, trying to remain out of the beast's range. She couldn't possibly take something like that down. She could only hit it once before she was exposed. It could only hit her once before she was done. But at least she could contain it here. She could stop this one from massacring any more of her people. Maybe she could even occupy it long enough for Virgil and Dove to accomplish their task, whatever it had become, before they withdraw. *If* they withdrew. The wolf turned away from her as it circled around the other side of the fountain. It seemed to freeze, as though spotting something in the distance. Time to go.

Her cloak flew back as she ran. Snow flung behind her every step. She squeezed her fist once more. The blade clicked. The wolf turned. Its red eyes landed upon her. They burned through the darkness covering her own. She locked on with her stare. She dashed onward as fast as she could. She leapt over the fountain basin. The black center of the wolf's eyes focused onto her. It started to growl.

It was like kicking a concrete wall. She felt the impact through every bone in her foot, along her lower leg, within the joint of her knee, and into her thigh so heavily that she thought it might break again. Wind struck her as the hulking beast rocked backward. She landed one quick strike into its side. She dove away as his tree-trunk arm streaked toward her. She made a short slash across its leg. The wolf threw a backhanded swipe. She tumbled away, then popped to her feet, opening her hand to withdraw the blade. She placed her bare palm out to vault over the beast's shoulder, using its own momentum to fling herself up. She clenched her fist. The blade scraped along the back of the wolf's neck as it twisted, trying to catch her. She rounded off to land on the edge of the fountain basin. She sprang to the top of the waterspout, sliding a moment before catching her balance. She saw the other cloak there, her brother, broken backward over the fountain rim. Bones and entrails peeked through long gashes along his chest and belly. His eyes were open. No shadow covered them. She squatted at top of the fountain.

The wolf growled in anger and pain. Snow stuck to the clumped points sticking from its fur. The cuts she'd made—the scratches that marked her best attempt at hurting it—were already closing.

"Kill you," it snarled, long streaks of drool hanging from its jaws. "Kill you all."

Riley used her perch to survey her surroundings. Fights continued in other areas of the park. Combatants raged in their own struggles between life and death. The wolf stared up at her. They were alone.

She stood up straight, towering over the wolf for

the first and possibly last time ever. She shook her bladed hand. Blood drops tapped onto the snow beneath her.

"We aren't hunters," she said, as much to herself as to the wolf below her.

The wolf growled.

"We're watchers. We're guardians."

The wolf crouched.

"We were supposed to be," she muttered.

She saw the vibration in the furry spikes along the beast's shoulders. She launched herself forward from the top of the fountain. She tucked her legs into a somersault. Momentum carried her into a second one before the ground rushed to meet her. She tucked into a roll along the ground. She stuck out one foot to twist back.

The wolf collided with the top of the fountain. It slammed off the spout and fell into the snow within the pool. It shoved itself up and nearly stumbled against the basin rail. Its breath puffed out in a thick fog. Its motions were wild. Wild made it sloppy. Sloppy made it easy to avoid.

She shifted before the wolf could leap at her again. She dodged claws flying like haymakers. She remembered the way Dove danced around the four wolves behind the fence that night, how she'd spin and dip and strike. Riley slipped away. Dove made it look so easy. Riley would need distance. As long as there was room to move, there was room to avoid it. If she could avoid the strike, she could land her own. She could be Bruce Lee fighting Kareem Abdul-Jabbar, if Abdul-Jabbar were six hundred pounds of savage muscle.

Riley slid back a step as the wolf took another swing. She popped the blade on her arm and drew back for her own strike. A claw flashed toward her. Her back wrenched as she tried to twist away. The tips of its claws ripped through her cloak sleeve. Razor blades tore through her arm. She flinched from the series of burning stings. Blood leaked through the wounds. She was exposed.

The wolf rushed toward her, claws flailing and teeth snapping. She dove to the ground as the beast lunged once again. Spit flew from its jaws. A roar rumbled through its throat. Its eyes followed her.

Riley slid out of her roll, planting her feet and one hand to spring again. The wolf rebounded off the ground and back at her. She dodged once more. And once again. She didn't even try landing any strikes of her own. Avoiding was difficult enough now that she'd been spotted. She bounced from the ground to the fountain rim, to the spout, to the pool, to the benches, and back, as the wolf slammed around every obstacle in its path. She spun to avoid another attack. Other shapes came into her view. More wolves.

The air shook as the wolf pulled its arm back for another looping swing. Riley kicked the side of its leg. It crumbled as its knee buckled inward. She jumped onto the fountain rim and up the spout once more, then squatted low as the wolf rose to recover. The other three approached.

The wolf growled loudly as it stared up at her once again.

"Stop," she heard, "please."

One of the other wolves held its arms out from its sides. All three of the newcomers were smaller than the first, but this one was noticeably thinner as well, wider through the hips and smaller through the shoulders. The fur on its face swept up and hung down more like that of a bobcat than a wolf. Its eyes were light red, not the deep blood hue of the other two, who continued to stare at her from beyond the edge of the fountain. Riley's view darted between them.

"Mr. Zarker," the thinner one said in a voice that seemed vaguely feminine under the snarl.

The large one—Zarker was apparently its name—held out its claws. Blood had soaked into the grooves of its nails and the palms of its hands. Some of that blood was hers. The pain was already fading from her arm. She glanced toward the thinner one. Its palms remained outstretched, as though trying to separate the two of them. The other two wolves lingered a step behind on either side. They waited. They watched her watch them.

"Riley," the thin one said, a rolling growl in her voice.

Riley narrowed her eyes at it. Its eyes and cheeks were wide, almost feline. There was concern on its face as it stared up at her halfway between the fountain and the northern path.

"Samantha," the wolf said, patting its chest.

"Samantha," Riley repeated. Her jaw slackened with realization. Mrs. Wallace had said that Riley wouldn't have the chance to call her that. Riley shook her head. The sides of her hood waved at the ends of her peripheral vision. The cloth in front rubbed against her nose.

"Not supposed to be like this," Riley said. "We were supposed to watch. To protect."

"Not anymore," Samantha replied.

Heavy breaths poured from Zarker as he

continued to stare. His claws remained out but restrained, as though held back by Samantha's presence.

"He didn't tell me it would be like this," Riley said. "I never agreed to a slaughter. We aren't hunters."

Samantha shook her head. Her sigh came out as thin steam. "Is he here?" Samantha looked from Riley to Zarker.

"Inside," Zarker said, pointing his chin to the museum behind Riley. His voice was so broken it made Riley's throat ache.

Riley checked the surrounding battlefield once more. There were more wolves now, fewer cloaks still moving. Bodies littered the edges of the plaza and the path that ran through it. The snow was more red than white. And still they continued fighting. Wolves swung claws. Humans swung swords. Wolves snapped their jaws. Humans stabbed their blades. Their steps were heavy with fatigue. None of them stopped. They were all rushing after death.

"Virgil," Riley said quietly.

"Inside," Samantha said, the word rolling and rising at the end like a question. "Dove."

Riley nodded.

Samantha closed her eyes. She shook her long head with another sigh.

"Riley," she said. "Always a good girl. Some bad choices." She looked up at Riley. Her eyes seemed almost sympathetic. As sympathetic as those of a monster could be. She looked across to Zarker. "Can't help you," Samantha said. "Not anymore."

Samantha's arms dropped to her sides. She tilted her head to sniff the air, then turned to the two wolves behind her. One was noticeably smaller than the other, its fur shorter and softer. It looked like a puppy compared to the other, with its thicker hair and more angled build.

"Keep them out," Samantha said. She lowered her head. "Riley," she said, nose pointed down. "Sorry."

Samantha sprang forward into a run, her strides

long. Snow flew up behind her. Riley glanced down to where Zarker jolted side to side. He was a predator eager to be let out of the cage. A series of puffs followed where Samantha rushed down the path toward the parking lot.

"Mine," Zarker growled from below. A smile seemed to break across his lips.

"Not anymore," Riley replied.

She wheeled around, jumped straight off the top of the fountain, then bounced off the edge of the pool and around the body broken over the side. She hit the ground with one footstep and began running with the next.

CHAPTER 9

SHAYERA WAS A TRAILING FLASH IN FRONT OF him. Her steps were soft pats on the hardwood floor. She darted left and right through the open area of the main gallery.

Nate tried to keep up. Rows of the exhibits blurred past. He felt a heaviness in the way he moved, lumbering, compared to the ease with which Shayera bounded forward. Light streams of smoke dotted gaps in the scent of the wall at the far end of the room.

He heard her feet scratch the floor. She jumped straight ahead. One of the guards dropped. A quick rip. The scent of sweat and blood exploded out. The other guard reacted. The combination of smoke scent and no scent twisted toward him. There was the familiar click of the blade.

Nate was on him in a second. The figure became clearer as he dug his claws in. The thick stench stung his nostrils. Rips in the cloak gave him form. Each cut made the target clearer until Nate saw the body painted in red beneath him.

He stopped.

Gore dripped from the sharpened edges of his nails. The liquid leaked between the scale-like skin of his palms. The scent was so dense he could barely separate where the blood ended and his hands began.

A dark cloud covered the guard's chest, soaking through the remaining fabric, sweeping around his sides, pouring to the floor. Jagged lines tore through him. He was more meat than man, now. His head remained a near-invisible void except for a single strip over his eyes. They were wet, open.

Adrenaline and testosterone were heavy in the dead man's blood. Panic and youth. Nate reached to pull the cloth from the man's face. He leaned in to smell. Flowery soap covered the young man's skin. A faint scent of peanut butter rimmed his lip and a sharp hint of aftershave came from his chin and neck, as though he'd cleaned up just for this night. The odor wasn't particularly familiar, nor was it particularly unfamiliar. He might have been from another town. Or they might've passed each other in the hallway at school, or on the street, in another life.

"Come on," Shayera whispered. She braced one arm on the door into the next gallery. "One more," she said.

On the floor behind her was a massacre. A metallic odor streamed up like dust after a bomb was dropped. Cracked bones poked through skin. The scent of blood was so thick it was nearly opaque in his mind. It felt as though the blood itself, the particles dispersed in the air, lodged themselves in his nostrils, seeping down his throat and into his lungs. There was just . . . so much blood.

"Move," Shayera growled. She pushed him hard on the shoulder.

The mechanism inside the metal bar across the door was softer this time. The path through the second gallery was narrower, with a lower ceiling. There was less room to maneuver.

Nate ignored the traces of glass, wood, old paint, the odor of his own kind still lingering from days before, and the overwhelming stench from those fallen around him. He keyed in on the absence of scent with thin trails of smoke and ash. A ghost wandered back and forth at the end of the galley. Nate slinked to the other side of the double doors. He heard a soft footstep, the whoosh of cloth, then a hollow echo before another step.

"Her," he said. The heat in his chest came on quick. It was familiar. It was comforting. Nate felt the skin pull back from his teeth. The red tint built in his eyes.

"No."

Nate's view darted to Shayera.

"Too angry," she said. "Too sloppy."

He snarled at her.

"On the street. Angry. Made you lose control."

Nate grunted as he tried to form words. He snorted. "Distracted," he said at last, one of the only words he could get out. "Not now."

"Ulrich," she replied. She was the smooth yellow of calm. "You," she continued. "More important than me."

Nate growled.

"I stop her," Shayera said. "You get him."

He showed her his teeth.

"Stop them here," she said. "Help Ulrich. More important."

She didn't move. She didn't even seem to breathe. He remembered the zigzag path that followed her across the gallery floor, the efficiency with which she'd torn through the guard a moment ago. She hadn't hesitated. She'd done the same at the train tracks, pulling Dove away from him, holding off a gang of blackrobes with only Zarker by her side.

Nate felt a phantom pain in his hand and shoulder. Dove. The giggle that echoed in his mind at night. The bouncing lunatic that had stalked him for months. His father had taken her leg. She'd taken his life. His father, High Councilor, alpha. Nate was not that. Not yet.

She'd still killed him.

"Fine," Nate said at last.

Shayera didn't move.

"Fine," he said again.

Shayera nodded. "Good. Remember that." She pressed her arm against the metal bar. "Wait and then go."

She pushed the door open and flew through.

Nate closed his eyes to follow her scent across the gallery. Shayera raced straight ahead. There was a metal click and a hard, hollow step. Shayera stopped. She growled loudly. The reply was a giggle.

Dove was a wisp. Shayera was an easy flow of adrenaline. She shifted back and forth, fluid as water. Shayera swung short, slashing strikes at smoke trails. She dodged whizzing stabs. Dove was heavy-soft steps on the wood, the rustle of cloth, the occasional high-pitched laugh.

"Nate!"

The voice seemed to echo from behind the main entrance.

There was a short slicing sound. Iron misted the air. Shayera let out a brief whimper as she pulled back her bloodied arm. A laugh. Rhythmic clicks. Nate shoved the door and rushed in.

He roared as he charged. The sound vibrated through the massive chamber of his chest and the round pipe of his throat. He felt it shake his entire body. His heart pumped lava. His feet slammed on the floor as he barreled toward the void dotted with vapor and a bloodied blade. He readied his claws and teeth. He wanted her blood. The ghost spun away. He twisted and slipped, sliding into a wall of old, painted wood, metal wiring, and pipes. Two picture frames dropped to the floor several feet down, glass shattering on impact.

Dove giggled.

Nate shoved off the wall. He searched for her, the leftover smoke that clung to the outside of her long cloak. She was the corner pieces of a new puzzle, none of its interior yet found. She withdrew her blade. Shayera's blood dripped from Dove's hand. His mind whispered that it was a trap. The rest of him screamed to attack.

He threw a wide swing from the left. Nothing but air. He threw an uppercut right. Spiraling scent. He lunged into looping strikes. Giggle. He growled, spun, snapped jaws. She was intangible. "Go!" he heard in a jagged feral tone.

There was the hollow metal tap on the wooden floor, the click and whir of the blade, a flutter of wind. He jumped again.

"Go!" he heard repeated. The sound bounced off something between him and Shayera. The blood had already stopped on her arm. Its scent flowed around an unseen object. "I can—"

"Go!" Shayera roared. The sound again suggested the shape of—"Remember!"

Nate stepped back. He pressed his hand against the wall until he felt the smooth metal bar into the final room. The scent trail shot toward him. Dove charged. A mechanical click. A banging foot step. A booming metal echo. Shayera leaped forward as well, adrenaline shooting through her. Nate shoved hard against the door. Dove was an outline hovering over him as he fell across the threshold. He saw the tip of her blade angle to him. Straight at his face. A small drip of blood clung to its tip, like the first night, when it stared at him through a hole in the back of his hand. That was how it all started.

The blade stopped. It inched back.

Shayera's glowing mass blew over the empty space where she pulled at Dove's leg. He saw the outline of the hood over her head. The tip of the blade waved inches from his face. Shayera pulled her back by the foot. Nate wanted to grab the blood-dotted metal on Dove's arm. He wanted to rip it off and shove the blade through Dove's own throat. Then he remembered.

Nate crawled beyond the doorframe. He pushed the door closed. Shayera softened behind it. Dove disappeared.

Short breaths filled the room with familiar scents. Wooden walls and filing cabinets, metal frames and handles, thousands of musty papers inside the drawers, the lingering scent of people from when they used to gather here, dust and mildew beneath the flowery odor killers placed on the cabinets and sprayed over the tapestries in the round meeting chamber further down the hall. He winced as the bright spot appeared in his mind.

There were two heartbeats in the records room. One hard and fast. One calm.

"What do you want with it?" Ulrich asked.

Nate could barely see him through the bright spot emanating from Virgil's hood. The Eye of

Providence at the center of the spot over Virgil's head angled down but continued to stare. Nate felt the blood boil in his veins. He was ready to charge through the hall and around the corner into the records room, but the eye and the burning scent around it held him back as though repelled by it. He hadn't seen Virgil or the burning eye painted over his hood since the night Nate was first forced to change. Change in every way.

Virgil opened his cloak enough to let out the scents of leather and metal. A sheathed sword hung from his hip.

"You think this paper gives you dominion over this land?" Virgil's words rumbled out.

"This town was created as a sanctuary. It is ours."

The symbol turned with Virgil. The image was gone as the smell still wafted, following him like a smoke signal.

Nate crept forward.

"It was your place as well." Ulrich reeked of fear

and desperation. "The Order has always worked hand-in-hand with our people."

Virgil leaned to the side and bent down, looking at the drawers lining the back wall.

"Your predecessors—"

A creak followed Nate's next step.

"Are dead," Virgil growled. "As is the Order."

Another step closer to the passage into the records room.

"I—I don't understand."

"No longer can we remain hidden, Mr. Ulrich." Virgil straightened up. "No longer can we abide beasts corrupting this world." Dust flew from an opened drawer. "The Lord demands a penance be paid." The sweet smell of old, moldy paper waved as Virgil flipped through the files.

"The Accord made between—"

"Are you familiar with Exodus 21:17?"

"—our ancestors and the Order have stood for over two hundred . . . "

The flipping paused for a moment. Nate leaned

forward for another step. He was almost close enough to peek around the corner. The flipping resumed.

"How dare you defy the laws of the Nobilitate Nobis!"

"And how dare you defy the laws of our Creator." The flipping stopped again. "The same Creator who once attempted to rid the world of corruption," another spray of dust as a different folder opened, "only to see it spread in His absence."

Pages rustled.

"The Lord demands this curse be extinguished," Virgil said. He remained still. The light silhouetted him.

Ulrich leaned to see.

"Your blood is cursed."

The file shut.

"None are innocent."

Virgil spun from the drawer. The Eye of Providence returned.

"All must be punished."

A feral roar came from outside the hallway. Nate froze before backing up a step.

Ulrich started, "What was that?"

"It doesn't matter."

A flutter of motion. A swish of wind. A damp plunge. One slow breath gurgled, bubbled forth. A heavy thud on the ground. Ulrich collapsed to the ground. The scent of his blood rose from him.

Heat surged through Nate's body. He shook with rage. Razors slid from his fingertips.

He heard the shatter of a large glass pane. A million glass slivers burst out, releasing the sweet odor of old paper and felt beneath it.

The eye pulled backwards. Virgil's head emerged from under the hood. He stuffed the file into his cloak. He reached for another item. New scents emerged: plastic, thin and recent, gas contained within. Butane.

Nate snarled.

"All must be punished."

Riley heard the wind rushing into and over the hood. She weaved through the violence exploding around her. She bounced around a pair of bodies lying facedown with fresh snow flakes melting into hot wounds. She twisted to avoid the wild swing of one arm nearly as long as she was tall. She heard a howl behind her as one of her so-called brothers stabbed a distracted wolf. Not supposed to happen. Not like this.

Samantha was light brown with a sprinkle of gray against the white field. Bodies littered her path. Snow kicked up in her wake as she wove through the small engagements along the pathway ahead. Riley lost her briefly behind a raging wolf with a skunk stripe down its back. She huddled over the bush and fence separating the plaza from the parking lot. The museum beckoned from atop the snow-covered stairs. Several sets of footprints, some human and some not, tracked through the lot and up the steps. Samantha heaved up and down in her ascent. Riley hurried onward. A thin, pale body came into view as she hopped up the final step. An old woman lay with her bare back toward the sky. Her wrinkled skin had the bluish hue of freezing. The museum doors closed behind Samantha just as Riley hit them to push through.

"Nate!" Samantha yelled in a way that was more a howl than a scream.

Bits of dirt had settled into the carpet while a fine layer of dust had gathered over the glass covering the pictures on the wall of the museum lobby. They may not have been noticeable to anyone, but to her it looked as though the space hadn't been cleaned in months. Riley followed Samantha through the doors of the first gallery before they could close.

Fallen hair had gathered along the base of the gallery's display cases. The wooden floors had dulled, and several long scratches stood out. She couldn't be sure if that meant they were new, or if she hadn't been able to see them before. Water dotted several sets of footprints across the room with Samantha still running ahead. In the back, coming into Riley's focus as she sprinted on, lay two bodies flanking the rear door. A pair of long gashes ripped one across its chest. The other more closely resembled the remains of a meal than a human: exposed bones and shredded meat wrapped in a discarded napkin.

"Mrs. Wallace," Riley said quietly. She placed her hand out and slowed her approach.

Samantha turned. Black spots expanded in the center of her light red eyes as though focusing on Riley. A smooth layer of fur outlined the lithe muscles on the inside of her arm. Longer hairs extended into gentle wave-like crests riding from her forearm up to her shoulder. Her flexed fingers ended in semitransparent glass tipped with a fine edge. Hair continued down the line of her back as she stared at Riley while hunched behind the closed door. "Samantha," Riley said, uncertainty creeping into her tone.

It was the first time she'd taken a good, long look at one of them, without the blur and shake of a camera or fear. There were the swept-back eyes and ears, the black and circular nose crusted dry from the cold, the long whiskers on the lips that curled back, the two pairs of fangs. No wonder people millennia ago had declared them wolf.

"I didn't know," Riley said. "This . . . this . . . "

"Go," whispered a voice in the distance on the other side of the door.

Samantha growled. The skin on her nose scrunched as though angry. The fangs, the claws, the size, the way they moved faster and with greater power than any normal person ever could: she was fearsome. They'd have been the stuff of horror stories long before there were horror stories.

A door slammed in the next room.

Riley tugged at the cloth covering her face. She pulled her hood down. She tilted her head toward the door. A loud crash came from behind followed by a growl and a hollow tap.

"It's her," Riley whispered.

"I know," Samantha replied. The center of her eyes had grown small, the red around them darker.

"She'll kill you."

Another growl as Samantha stared at the door again. Behind it were the sounds of metal scraping on the wooden floor, animalistic grunts, snapping jaws, blades cutting the air, and laughter. Samantha kicked open the door. Splinters flew.

Blood dripped from Dove's blade. The end of her cloak flitted across the floor. Her hood bounced as she seemed to skip through the center aisle. A wolf staggered back from her, panting, head drooping as though heavy. It was long and lean, feminine, with sleek fur like a greyhound but black as a shadow. The only shadow in the room. Blood dripped from its claws, tracing down the inside of its arm.

"Sister Sapphira," Dove said, landing from one final skip. Her voice was high and joyful. "Join the game."

Samantha stalked forward. Riley rushed out in front of her.

"We have to stop," she said, throwing her arms out toward the two of them. "This is not our purpose."

"Cleanse the world," Dove said. She swayed in her stance. "Rid it of corruption." She straightened up. She stretched one leg out in front of her and bounced onto it. Riley heard the sleek shadow wolf step back as Dove hopped to the other side of the aisle. "Ours will be the names of the new Gospels."

Riley heard Samantha as an engine revving from behind and above her.

"Virgil is the corruption," Riley said, angling to keep her palms toward both Dove and Samantha, as Samantha had done outside to keep Zarker back. "He's corrupted our cause."

"Killing them *is* our cause." Dove swung her legs in backward steps, popping and releasing her blade with each footfall.

The engine roared.

"No. No, no. My father would have never done anything like this."

Dove stopped. The blade extending from her arm was caked with red. Riley looked into the gap between Dove's hood and the cloth stretched between its sides. Darkness covered her only hint of humanity. "Father Pius led us here," Dove said. "Every moment has brought us to this one. This is the path we are on."

The shadow backed to lean against one of the walkways branching from the center aisle.

"None may stray from the path chosen for them."

Virgil's voice rang in the back of Riley's head.

"High Councilor," said the black wolf. "Don't."

Samantha's growl had become an ambient noise in the room.

"He saved me, too, Sister," Dove said. "When the corruption took my family, it was Father Vigilius who gave me a new home. He led me from the darkness and into the light."

"This wasn't supposed to happen," Riley said yet again.

Dove shook her head. "This is exactly how it was supposed to happen."

Riley felt her arms lowering. She straightened and raised them again.

"Father Pius set us on this path, but he could not lead us on it. He had to get out of the way so that Father Vigilius might carry us home."

"What?" Riley said, letting her arms drop.

"There are no accidents, Sister."

A growl blasted over Riley so loud it made her eyes flutter.

"Please stay back," the shadow panted, "please."

Riley pulled at the strings tying her cloak at the neck. She pulled it open wide enough to expose the handle of the pistol holstered to her hip.

"What does that mean?"

"*Fata viam invenient.*"

A roar filled the room. Riley turned just as Samantha shoved past her.

Dove giggled as she backpedaled.

The shadow lunged forward. Dove dodged away. Samantha jumped in, spit flying as she roared. Dove dodged again. Samantha swung madly. Dove spun away. She leapt toward the greyhound that staggered ahead. There was a whir as Dove's blade sliced the air. A flash of blood followed. The greyhound stumbled to the side. Blood flooded down its legs. Samantha charged on. Dove giggled as she flipped backwards and away. Samantha swung heavy blows with each step. Dove still bounced, remaining just out of Samantha's charge. Samantha stuttered her step, delaying her next swing. She swung as Dove landed from another jump. The claw launched toward her. Dove's blade rose in a flash. Samantha howled in pain. Dove spun away yet again, as though nothing had happened. Samantha shook her right arm at the shoulder. The arm hung as deadweight. The greyhound struggled to right itself on the floor.

Dove resumed her bouncing stride through the

center of the room. She circled to the rear, toward the door to what Riley always assumed was a large storage area.

"Useless," she said. "Getting in the way."

The greyhound crawled back to push itself against the wall. "Stay back," it panted, "stay back." Samantha continued shaking her arm, watching as Dove paced in front of the door as though patrolling it.

"Father Pius," Dove continued, "in the way."

Her right hand twitched at the wrist. The blade extended and withdrew with every motion.

"No accidents."

Riley's teeth clenched. Her nostrils flared.

"Should have watched you burn."

She moved toward the other side of the room from where Samantha and the greyhound were recovering. She remembered the sting of shattered glass slicing across her face. Dove must've been there that night. Why wouldn't she be?

"Like that useless boy."

That was the only way she'd know.

Riley stepped forward and glanced at Samantha, who met her eyes and nodded with a low, stuttering growl.

Virgil had lied to her. Lied about the whole thing. Nate . . . Nate was right.

"Sister Sapphira," Dove said, playfully swaying as she paced in front of the door.

Riley squeezed her fist. The blade shot from the gauntlet strapped to her arm.

"Join the game."

Nate closed his eyes as he took one long inhalation through his nose. Virgil's hood remained pulled back. The light from the hood still covered some of Nate's vision, but a much clearer picture came to him: Virgil's tall and thin figure, the sword at his side, Ulrich in a pool of blood on the floor, the wooden table with the shattered glass over the mildewed paper of the charter, and the spark of a tiny flame within Virgil's hand.

Ulrich didn't even try to change. He didn't attempt to defend himself. For all his talk of building for the future and regaining what had been lost, he'd dropped to the floor as if there were no longer anything worth fighting for. Maybe there wasn't. Since the fence went up, he'd spent most of his days in meetings. The Council might have been all he had left. Then Nate had taken that away from him, turned their attention to him. He'd lost his last reason to live.

The flame lowered to the musty pages in the felt-lined case.

Nate lowered his shoulder as he rushed around the corner like a linebacker chasing the quarterback. His footsteps pounded through the small room. The flame ignited on the edge of the paper. Nate charged.

He launched one claw forward. His fingertips shredded across cloth and skin. Virgil grunted from the blow. New blood filled the air. Different, yet similar. An animal scent lingered within it. Nate thrust his other claw into Virgil's side. His nails scraped along the old man's ribs. The light from the hood hanging over Virgil's back made him a silhouette framed by a glow that burned Nate's senses. His entire body was burning. He smelled the smoke. He roared as Virgil staggered back, banging against drawers lining the rear wall. Nate shook the blood from his fingers. Drops hit the ground like rain.

"Too late," creaked a voice from within the silhouette. "The path is set."

Nate shoved his huge hands forward. He slammed Virgil back. The wooden drawers cracked from the force.

"No," Virgil exhaled. "No."

Nate dug his claws into the old man's shoulders. He pulled in to slam back once more. Drawers of files cracked and collapsed around Virgil's frame.

"Not you," Virgil muttered.

Nate roared once more. Globs of spit showered

over Virgil's darkened face, so obscured that he appeared more an abstract than an object. Nate felt himself burning, inside and outside.

Virgil choked out words. "You do not get this honor."

Nate stepped back. He swung short strikes at the fumes of light and blood and smoke and splintered wood streaming in front of him. Some grazed and some cut, some deeply. Nate continued swinging. Little resistance met his claws. A fog built up in his mind. He swung out of instinct and memory, the pattern in his mind. He stomped at where he knew Virgil to be. Savage breaks met each blow. His final roar vibrated through his body. He stepped back. A sharp scent stung his nose. Burning hair.

Smoke had filled the room around him. The fire cast bright heat in all directions. He staggered back. He waved his hands, trying to push away the haze that flooded his mind and overwhelmed his senses. It was exactly what had happened outside, where the fires were meant to obscure the blackrobes' invasion of the plaza. Nate felt a heat in his bones, hotter than that which emanated from the flames, spreading over the table to the other drawers lining the walls. He wanted to pounce onto Virgil once more—what was left of him—and bury his claws in the dead flesh. He wanted to rip out the old man's heart. But the smoke filled his breath. He stumbled back. His feet knocked against something solid but soft. He nearly tripped trying to avoid Ulrich's body on the floor, flames already creeping up the leg of his pants. Nate gagged. Smoke puffed out from his lungs. Everything was heat. He backed out of the room. He needed to get out. Let Virgil burn. It was fitting that he would. Poetic in a way.

Nate ran one hand over the drawers as he rushed back toward the hall. The metal handles scraped at his fingers. He waved his other hand in front of him. It did nothing to clear the smoke from his sight or breath. He inhaled deeply. Little oxygen came. He bumped off the doorframe. He fell into the hall-way. He lashed out to catch himself, splintering the wooden drawers that lined the passage out. He gagged once more, hacking smoke from his lungs. He pressed on, hopping toward the door, pushing his hands and feet against the ground. He dug his claws in to continue on. His surroundings were cascading clouds of dark gray and black, thick as rock and brittle as ash. He'd seen this before. His hand bashed against something hard ahead. The door. He shoved one arm weakly against it. He did it again. Light broke through the dark.

Shayera was slumped on the ground to the side of the gallery's main aisle. She clutched at a long wound across her stomach. A thick trail followed Dove as she jumped around the room. Two masses followed her. Familiar scents. His mother and—

"Riley?" he said.

She seemed to freeze in the moment.

Her head was a red mask of rage and sweat. There was no trace of the familiar shampoo. There was little hair at all. Her arms and legs remained hidden the same way many of the others' were.

Leather and metal leaked where her cloak had been pulled open. A tang of gunpowder lingered just behind the cloak.

The moment passed.

"Help us!" Riley yelled.

His mother was a mass of adrenaline streaking behind Dove's trail of red smoke. She'd been hurt too. His mother. A dried line rode down her forearm.

The smoke and heat poured out behind him.

Dove, the glowing skull that burned into his mind. The cackling specter who taunted and hunted and wounded him. He focused on the trail behind her. The one who'd killed his father. Forced him to turn. Turned his best friend against him. And now, hurt his mother, the last person he had left in the world.

He traced Dove's movement as she dodged around the other two. She was always spinning, jumping, rolling, trying to turn her opponents around. He could use the others to push her toward him. He could find the pattern. He could strike her down.

A light emerged from within the smoke.

A glowing eye pierced his senses.

"You do not get this honor."

A sudden heat burst from the nape to the apple of his neck. Metal sliced through living meat. When he looked down, he saw the blade emerge from his throat as though he'd been skewered. He twitched and shook. Tired, he felt himself dropping. The blade pushed his jaw shut. There was little blood on the sword. A small clump of wet, red fur stuck to its tip. His breath leaked out around the blade as black clouds filled the space around him. He watched the world fade.

CHAPTER 10

RILEY WATCHED AS THE COLOR DRAINED FROM HIS eyes. His jaw slacked against the edge of the blade protruding from his throat. The fur covering his body jittered while he shook as though about to vomit. The red-tipped blade guided him down to his knees. His shoulders sagged and the back of his hands thumped heavily on the wooden floor. The blade withdrew. A single drop of blood formed through the short fur over his throat.

He lingered there. The hair on his face was short, neat, and softened against the strong, angular features beneath. His color was only slightly darker than he had as a person. The two pairs of fangs were visible as his mouth hung open. He slumped forward with the slightest sway. At any second he could blink himself back to awareness, the red filling in the black of his eyes. He could draw in breath. He could jump up to his feet.

Riley waited. He would lift his head to meet her gaze.

Then he collapsed. His head smacked against the floor.

The sword dropped from Virgil's hand as it exited the wound, clanging on the ground. Shallow scratches rode the contours of his face. His cloak was a shredded mess, dark stains filling what wasn't missing while the shreds of his white shirt were red and soaked against his body. His eyes met Riley's. She felt them lock like hooks into the sockets of her skull.

He could still stand. These wolves . . . wolves like him . . . they were strong. They could heal. They made her heal. They made her whole. They were made of strength. It was in their veins.

Samantha dropped to her knees nearby. Her mouth was wide with a scream that Riley saw but didn't hear. The shadow wolf struggled forward on its hands, dragging its legs behind. It reached one long, sleek arm toward where Samantha bent forward screaming once more.

Riley returned to Virgil's stare. One light blue pupil stood out against the intense red around it while the other nearly blended with the white of his eye. He stared at her as though trying to transfer a thought into her mind. "You were a fool," she imagined, "Stupid, broken little girl." Their eye contact broke as Virgil staggered to the side. Dove jumped in to catch him.

A single thin line curved from the blade onto the floor. The body remained bent over itself, leaning onto the head and one shoulder, one leg folded underneath. Dense brown fur rose in short hooks along his back. How long did it take for them to change back? Maybe he was still alive. He could still push himself up from the floor. He could still fight.

Riley's words rang in her mind. *I hope I never see you again.*

Samantha slammed one fist into the ground. The skin rose from around her locked jaw. She shook with rage. She inched to where Dove pointed her blade, one arm extended as Virgil draped over her. Dove's view darted across all of them, Samantha passing forward as she arose, the shadow wolf crawling across the floor, Riley frozen, and him. He didn't move.

I hope I never see you again.

She heard the water bubbling against the sides of the creek named for his father. The rocks were slick with water and moss. She looked up at him sitting on the stone that curved into the current. He stared into the ripples, followed the water as it flowed past. It was never deterred. She looked down as well. She saw herself standing on the creek bank. She was eleven then, maybe twelve. She wore the old army jacket that smelled vaguely of her father. She angled her view to the top of the rock. His shaggy hair was pushed behind his ears, before he started keeping it short. He remained perched on that rock, staring at the water as though miles away.

"Let's make a promise," she remembered saying.

He'd looked to her. The skin was heavy under his eyes.

"Let's promise that we'll never make each other feel bad."

He blinked. His expression lifted with surprise. "Okay," she remembered him saying, "I promise."

"Good," she'd replied. She'd felt as though she should smile, but she didn't. "Me too."

The body on the floor pulled into itself, the bones within it shrinking. The dense hair covering it retracted until all that remained was bare skin, plain and naked and fragile. She could see the rises and falls of bone beneath flesh, the ridges of spine that lined down its back leading to the light brown hair covering its head. The face remained tilted away.

She didn't want to see it. The red-rimmed hole remained through the back of his neck. A single red streak slowly gathered into a fold between neck and shoulder.

After all their promises, their jokes, their long, wandering talks about which movie actors were the coolest or the sexiest or would be the best to have as a mom or dad, their marathons of filmmakers or themes or periods or actors and actresses, his jokes about her and Remy, her jokes about him and Hailey, or Lauren, or Marianna, or whatever girl at their school he secretly had a crush on that year, her teasing him for driving slowly when she needed to get home after watching four straight Coen brother's kidnapping movies, sitting on the bench outside her old apartment building, staring at the stars and debating things they agreed on and making up stories about the strangers who wandered by . . . After all that, the last words she'd had to offer him were, "I hope I never see you again."

Samantha scratched deep lines into the floor as

the other wolf reached to pull her back. Dove kept her blade extended as she clung to Virgil's arm draped over her shoulder. She was his crutch. Virgil shook his head weakly, as though coming out of sleep. He met Riley's stare.

She felt the metal mass at her hip. It tugged at her belt. It weighed her down. She reached for it. Her hand wrapped about the handle of the pistol easily, like she'd done it a thousand times before, as though the grooves in the grip were molded specifically for her fingers. Virgil steadied himself on his own feet. He stared at Riley. The barrel stared back.

The blast shattered the silence.

Dove spun as the bullet hit her. Maybe her chest. Maybe her shoulder. The force threw her sideways. Virgil rocked as though someone had kicked the chair he tilted back in. He caught himself before falling. He straightened up. His stare was undeterred.

"You," Riley said to the black wolf, the gun in her left hand shaking in front of her, "get Samantha out of here."

The sleek wolf rose to its feet. It groped for Samantha's arm. Samantha snapped at the other wolf's hand.

"Go," Riley said, "both of you. Go."

Samantha snarled, staring at Dove and Virgil ahead. Dove used one arm to push herself up from the floor.

"Leave."

Virgil pointed his chin at Riley. Riley trained the gun on him.

"Samantha," Riley said. Virgil seemed to grow right in front of her. The shallow slices on his face had closed. "He's dead."

Samantha growled, snapping her jaws.

"Now get out."

Virgil glanced to the sword on the ground at his feet before returning his view to her. She locked her elbow again, securing the gun.

"Get out. Or you'll be dead too. Like everyone else," she said. "Like him."

Another snapping, broken growl.

"Get out!" Riley screamed. She turned the gun on Samantha. "Go!"

Samantha snarled at her. Her four fangs were as long and thick as Riley's thumbs and tapered into dull points still sharp enough to force their way through muscle.

"He's dead!" Riley yelled. She blinked at the water forming in her eyes. Her hand shook the gun in front of her. "Take her and go," she continued, looking at the black wolf tugging Samantha's arm. "You can't die, too." Riley's voice shook as much as the gun.

Dove slithered up to her feet. Her left arm hung at her side. She dabbed fingers at the wound in her collar.

The greyhound pulled at Samantha. "No," she snapped. "No, no."

"Mrs. Wallace," Riley said. She swayed the gun in front of her, uncertain of who to aim at as they all looked toward her. The muscles in her extended arm began to ache. "You need to go. Please."

"No," Samantha said again, trying to tear away from the greyhound.

"You need to live."

"High Councilor," the shadow wolf whispered, holding Samantha's arm in one hand and reaching its other hand over her shoulder. "Please."

Riley wiped her sleeve across her face. "You're the only one left."

The room had gone hazy as smoke poured out of the doorway behind Virgil. Orange flames licked from down the hall.

"Please, Samantha. I can't let you die too." Virgil and Dove were blurry in Riley's eyes. "I can't."

Samantha let out one last growl in protest as she withdrew. The shadow stepped in front of her like a bodyguard, eyeing Dove as the wolves backed from Riley's sight.

"Sister," Virgil said quietly.

The tattered cloth hung heavy with dried blood. She blinked away the tears so she could see him sharply. The scratches on his face crossed the lines she'd seen so many times before. Less of the cloak remained on his chest and sides than had been torn. A small cross peeked through a high rip. Blood dulled the shimmer of his shirt. He reached one hand out to her. His fingers were red and crusted.

"I see that you haven't forgotten," he said. His voice was jagged and muffled, as though the angles hurt coming out. He put one arm out for Dove. She caught his weight once again, wincing as he leaned on her. He wrapped his other arm around himself. "The anger. The grief. The guilt. They are your weapons."

Riley again wiped the water from her eyes. It came right back. The gun quaked in front of her. Her whole body shook. She heaved for breath. She heard the air in her lungs louder than the door slamming behind her.

"This was all for you, Sister Sapphira."

Flames lit the hallway behind him.

"All for you, Riley."

Dove eased Virgil on as he stepped forward.

"Everything I've done. Everything we've ever done. It was all to set you on this path. We are tools pointing you toward the fate our Lord has chosen. You are chosen."

She scrubbed her sleeve over her eyes. She steadied the gun in one hand as the other fumbled to pull the cloak off.

"Chosen to end the corruption."

She switched the gun between hands. She shook her shoulder free. The heavy garment dropped to the floor around her.

"You must lift this curse, Riley. Bring His favor once more."

She kicked at the cloak. It bunched on her foot. She kicked it again.

"Everything," Virgil said, "from the day you were born. It was all a part of His plan. You are His instrument. You are His redemption."

"Screw you!" she yelled, kicking the cloak free at last. She stomped on it before pushing it out with her foot. She stabbed the gun forward. "Screw you and screw your duty and screw your Lord!"

"You deny His plan, Sister, but you can't deny your part in it."

Her arm burned. Her chest rose and fell, the gun swaying with it.

Dove held Virgil through another uneasy step. She rubbed at the hole near her shoulder.

Riley inched back to keep distance.

"This is your fate, Sister."

Riley took another step back.

"You are beneath the shroud."

Another step. She outpaced them.

"Within the darkness cast upon this world."

Another.

"You will be bathed in the light."

She continued her steps back.

"None may stray."

Smoke flowed out from the doorframe in the distance. Virgil took a long step around the body in front of him. It was naked and pale and facedown, motionless. It was a lump on the ground. Meat and nothing more. Everything it had been—everything *he* had been—was gone. He wasn't there anymore. Not now. Never again.

She glanced over her shoulder as she retreated. The main door was only a few feet away. A few drops of blood marked where Samantha and the other wolf had pushed it open.

"These weapons I have given you, Sister."

She backed away faster.

She lowered the gun. She blinked away the last of her lingering tears.

"Use them."

She shoved her elbow back at the metal bar across the door. She threw her arm out, tossing the entrance open.

"And he that curseth his father or his mother . . ."

She stepped out of the room.

" . . . shall surely be put to death."

The door swung shut. It closed with a heavy slam.

They were gone.

All of them.

Gone.

CHAPTER 11

THE FIRES HAD STARTED TO DIE DOWN. THE smoke calmed into thin drifts through gentle snow. The tracks had almost vanished, spots of blood half-covered, bodies flaked white. Few combatants remained standing. Most were still. Riley heard whimpers over the crunch of snow as she ran down the stairs.

Samantha had folded over at the base of the stairs. She reached out as though trying to climb, but without the strength to move. The black greyhound held her back with one arm around her midsection.

Samantha was halfway across the lot when Riley jumped from the final set of steps.

"You!"

The black center of Samantha's red eyes narrowed onto Riley.

"You brought them here!"

Riley froze at the foot of the long staircase.

The sleek wolf wrapped both its arms tightly around her as Samantha tried to wiggle away. She threw an elbow, hitting the healing wound on the greyhound's side. It groaned. Samantha sliced across its arm. She kicked away.

Riley dropped to one knee in the snow. She bowed as heavy steps rushed toward her, stopping inches from her face. Hot breath buffeted the top of her head. It rustled her short hair and heated her neck and down the collar of her shirt.

"I did," she said. "I brought them here."

Samantha roared. Spit drizzled over Riley's skull.

"If we weren't friends," she mumbled just over the sound of the rage pouring from Samantha's throat. "Maybe . . . " Sharp growls met Riley's words. " . . . maybe none of this would have happened. Maybe—"

A brick cracked into the side of Riley's face. The impact tossed her to the ground.

Samantha snarled over her. Tapered teeth and long fangs filled Riley's vision. She glanced up to the blood-red eyes swallowing their black centers. Samantha roared once more, tossing her clawed hands outward. Riley drew in one long, final breath. Samantha thrust herself forward. She collapsed to the ground.

Samantha scratched at the layer of snow. She buried her snout into the short hair on the back of her hands. Her cries were the high-pitched whine of an animal caught in a trap. She pushed her nose into the snow.

"Councilor," the greyhound said as it approached, stark black against the white.

Samantha rolled over herself, trembling with grief, guilt, and anger at the same time.

Riley knew those feelings well. She pushed herself up from the ground. She rubbed at her face, surprised the skin hadn't been split open. She moved her jaw to test if it still worked. The pain was already fading as she brushed snow from her cheek. It was a bit colder now without the cloak—exposed—but not as cold as she would have expected. Chilly rather than frozen.

"Councilor," the greyhound said once more as it crouched to place one hand on the curve of Samantha's spine. "We have to go. We need to get you away from here."

Riley stepped away.

Samantha rubbed her nose into the ground as though burrowing. She released a high, stuttering whine.

"We need to keep you safe."

"They're still here," Riley said. "You need to leave."

Red eyes lifted from the snow. Riley remained still as Samantha rose up in front of her, her eyes so intense they were nearly blinding. Her vision darkened as Samantha's hands came to clamp both sides of Riley's head.

"I'm sorry," she muttered. "It was me. I did it."

The hands gently pulled her forward. Their heads pressed together. A deep exhale warmed the space between them. There was a hint of copper to the breath. Samantha grasped the base of Riley's neck. The skin of the wolf's palms were a thousand rough points against Riley's bare flesh. Another breath warmed her face before Samantha pulled away.

Samantha's eyelids drooped. The central black had returned. She kept one hand on the base of Riley's neck as she stood and turned toward the other—the sleek, black greyhound.

The three of them walked across the rest of the parking lot, toward the distant growls and grunts and screams that still popped from those who didn't know the fight was over. They walked together through the opening in the fence and around the bodies blanketed in fresh snow, some cloaked and some bare. Their spilled blood had diluted to pink.

A distant, mechanical rumble echoed off the buildings, faint and heavy like an avalanche.

"Guard is coming," the greyhound said.

Samantha nodded.

A pair of large bodies flashed across the path ahead, passing the fountain in the center of the plaza.

"Shayera," Samantha said in a soft, almost whispered tone. "Find who you can. Tell them to go home right now."

Riley glanced back at the tracks descending the museum steps. Her short and shallow footsteps crossed the deep, long drags of Samantha and her companion, Shayera. She saw the indentations of where she and Samantha had fallen, their impact mixing together as one large disruption. The tracks blurred together before beginning anew, parallel to each other. The rumble grew louder. She heard a growl as she returned to the path ahead.

Zarker eyed her from behind another pair of wolves.

"They're coming," said one of the others. The last of the skirmishes had stopped. There were no more sounds of struggle. One wolf remained slumped on the ground just off the path leading out of the park. A curled, naked body was half buried in front of it.

"Can't be here."

The rumble shook the top layer of snow.

"That one," said Zarker, his lips curling as he spoke. "That one is mine."

"You will not touch her," Samantha replied.

Zarker snorted disapproval, fixing his eyes on Riley. "They come here," he said, "They kill us. And you let them live."

"Nothing to fight for," Samantha said.

"The High Councilor?" said the other wolf, one with a black spot over its left eye that vaguely resembled a spade.

Samantha shook her head.

"Nathaniel?"

"We must go," Samantha replied.

"Go where?" Zarker spat toward the other two. "Stuck in this fence."

"Can't be here," said the one with the spade.

"Hide then," Zarker growled. He looked at Riley. "Can't keep them out." He looked toward the others. "Can't keep us in."

"Nowhere else to go," said the spade.

"No more!" Zarker shouted, taking a step back from the others. "No more!" He unleashed one angry grunt as he turned and stomped away. Rows of sharp points lined his back in the most savage, jarring way possible.

"Councilor Maier," Samantha said.

The spade turned from watching Zarker walk away.

"Tell anyone left to go home."

"Yes, High Councilor," he said. He took a step back. He bowed before withdrawing. The third wolf followed him, glancing to where Zarker had wandered.

A vibration shook through Riley's foot. She leaned to see a large vehicle in desert camouflage roll down the road on the far side of the plaza.

"Riley."

Snow continued to fall around her. A faint trail of smoke peeked over the top of the museum, its origin so far back that it disappeared.

"Where do you want to go?"

Bodies sunk into snow like soft beds. They were still as sleeping. Lost in dreams. Nothing bad could happen to them ever again.

"With you."